STAR CROSSING

How to Get Around in the Universe

Books by Judith Herbst:

SKY ABOVE AND WORLDS BEYOND
BIO AMAZING
ANIMAL AMAZING
STAR CROSSING: HOW TO GET AROUND IN THE UNIVERSE

STAR CROSSING:

★

How to Get Around in the Universe

Illustrated with photographs
and diagrams

★   ★   ★

JUDITH HERBST

ATHENEUM 1993 NEW YORK

MAXWELL MACMILLAN CANADA
TORONTO

MAXWELL MACMILLAN INTERNATIONAL
NEW YORK OXFORD SINGAPORE SYDNEY

The diagrams on pages 145, 154, and 177 are by Richard Rosenblum.

Atheneum
Macmillan Publishing Company
866 Third Avenue
New York, NY 10022

Maxwell Macmillan Canada, Inc.
1200 Eglinton Avenue East
Suite 200
Don Mills, Ontario M3C 3N1

Macmillan Publishing Company is part of the Maxwell Communication Group of Companies.

FIRST EDITION
PRINTED IN THE UNITED STATES OF AMERICA
2 4 6 8 10 9 7 5 3 1

THE TEXT OF THIS BOOK IS SET IN PALATINO
BOOK DESIGN BY SIGNET M DESIGN, INC.

Library of Congress Cataloging-in-Publication Data
Herbst, Judith.
Star crossing : how to get around in the universe / by Judith Herbst; illustrated with photographs and diagrams.—1st ed.
p.   cm.
Includes bibliographical references.
Summary: Discusses the scientific developments and theoretical concerns that have led to current achievements in space exploration and will be necessary for future space travel.
ISBN 0–689–31523–6
1. Outer space—Exploration—Juvenile literature.   2. Astronautics in astronomy—Juvenile literature.   [1. Astronautics.
2. Interstellar travel.   3. Outer space—Exploration.]   I. Title.
QB500.22.H47   1992
919.9'04—dc20   92–8475

This book is dedicated

to the memory of my physics teacher

at Bayside High School,

who thought I'd never understand this stuff.

ACKNOWLEDGMENTS

★

*I*f this book is good, it's because I got a lot of special help from the following people. Now I get to thank them in print: Dr. Robert Bussard, for his patience and expertise and for forcing me to use the phone; L. J. Carter from the British Interplanetary Society; Rolland and Mary Cormier, for sharing my enthusiasm; Diane Dickey at Kellogg's; Douglas Egan, who provided a wonderful Einstein photo; John W. Macvey, for his analogy; Professor John M. McKinley, whose computer-generated star fields knocked my socks off; Peter Nicholls, who, from Australia, pointed me in the right direction for the cover picture; Fred Rick at Los Alamos, for going above and beyond; Robert Romer at the *American Journal of Physics;* Rick Sternbach, for coming through with a fabulous rocket when I was most desperate; and all the librarians who filled my sometimes oddball requests for obscure journals and out-of-print books.

I couldn't have done it without you.

CONTENTS

★

STAR CROSSING

★

How to Get Around in
the Universe

CHAPTER 1

★

It's Not as Easy
as It Looks

W ow!" we all said.

The TV screen flickered in the unfamiliar black and white.

"Down two-and-a-half . . . forward forty feet. Picking up some dust . . . thirty feet . . ."

"We copy you, *Eagle*."

A quarter of a million miles away Mission Control held its breath. For a moment there was no sound at all . . . from the men in white shirts, sleeves rolled carelessly to the elbows; from the starry-eyed audience that stretched all the way around the globe; from the tiny moon craft that floated softly to rest.

"Houston?"

My God! we thought. They sound so close!

"Tranquility Base, here. The *Eagle* has landed."

Mission Control exploded like party-goers on New Year's Eve who see the past suddenly drop away. The cheers echoed through the hallways and perhaps still remain, drifting among the computer hardware. The ghosts of *Apollo 11*.

We heard a faint chatter from deep inside the moon machine as the spacemen from planet Earth prepared to open the hatch. Buck Rogers in a minivan made by Grumman. The talk was all marvelously, mysteriously technical gibberish to those of us wearing sneakers and chewing Bazooka. But the following day and for weeks to come, we would all be able to recite the litany of space travel, word for incomprehensible word.

The minutes stretched to eternity while the three voyagers checked and double-checked the systems and bored us all to death. We wondered why it was taking so long. We shifted in our seats, waiting . . . waiting . . .

And then at last the hatch opened.

Motionless, now, our hearts stopped in midbeat, we watched in awe from our couches, our BarcaLoungers, the street in front of the appliance store where ten RCA Victors showed us the man in the moon.

We had finally made it. We were on another world, 240,000 miles away. A world with no water and no air and a strange geology—dusty, boulder-stewn, and oddly dimpled like some big, gray golf ball. We are spacers, all of us thought. We are star travelers.

But we were not.

The ship we had watched lift off from Cape Canaveral on that warm July day was not really a ship at all. Underneath its muscles, underneath the grand and sweeping presidential promises and NASA hype, the *Saturn V* was nothing more than three fuel tanks and a collection of engines. It hauled the little *Apollo* spacecraft up and through Earth's atmosphere like a team of sweating oxen, roaring and snorting and gasping flame until the air ran out and the sound waves melted away. Filled to the brim with heavy liquid propellant, the three stages went nowhere except into the ocean when their cargo of fuel was expended.

Alone in the silence, the *Apollo* capsule drifted toward the moon, no bigger than a grain of sand in the deep and endless void. Its three cramped passengers shifted and twitched, confined to their tiny space car with one window and exploding bolts. Without access to showers and toilet facilities,* eating pastes and liquids from plastic bags, they went where they were carried—the highly trained, overqualified keepers of the robot. A billion electronic neurons assembled back home guided the astronauts to their target—measuring the fuel, firing the engines, choosing the landing site. And they told the three adventurers when it was time to leave.

"Wait!" the astronauts might have wanted to say. "Wait! Let's not go home yet. Let's go to Mars!"

But they couldn't, because that kind of space travel was still too fancy for us. So they arrived and departed exactly as their program dictated, and a week later they fell from the sky like a meteor into the cold, watery arms of Mom and Pop Earth. We fished them out and dried them off and pinned medals on their chests because they were the first men on the moon.

Like children, we left our space toys everywhere, hardly used and thrown away. The lunar module sits silently on the Sea of Tranquility, frozen in time and patiently waiting. The tanks of the *Saturn V* are space junk, retrieved from the ocean but never to see service again. And the *Apollo* capsule rests like the bones of a dinosaur in the Smithsonian Institution in Washington, D.C.

No, we are not space travelers, but, oh, how desperately

---

*Don't get nervous. The astronauts' suits were specially designed to take care of waste elimination.

---

we want to be! From the time of the ancient Greeks, from biblical Ezekiel, maybe, and long, long before, human beings have looked to the stars and dreamed of capturing them. Crude paintings on the walls of deep, cool caves show us that people were very much aware of the stars many thousands of years ago. They noticed too the phases of the moon, the advance of certain very bright stars, and the daily motion of the sun. Certainly they witnessed the sudden and spectacular plunge of meteors and the curious appearance of comets. They knew that something wondrous was going on up there, but for these earliest of peoples, it was all far beyond their grasp.

With the rise of civilization came daring ideas. In A.D. 130 or so, the Greek writer Lucian proposed an unusual way to travel to the stars. In his book *A True History*, a sailing ship is swept up by a furious whirlwind at sea and deposited in outer space. The ship then cruises among floating islands while the crew takes in the curious sights. High tech this wasn't, but Lucian's typhoon bears a remarkable resemblance to today's rotating black holes, a hypothetical space shortcut proposed by some scientists (more about that in Chapter 10).

The really good rocket designs did not appear in print until Jules Verne (1828–1905) came along. Right around this time hot-air ballooning had become quite popular, and some of the more slapdash SF writers figured they'd just adapt the balloons to outer-space travel. But not Verne, whose stories offered up a grand array of star vehicles. His most famous ship is *Columbiad*, the cone-shaped moon craft in his novel *From the Earth to the Moon*. Verne predated NASA's *Apollo* by one hundred years, but it was almost as though he had seen the future. No wonder he came to be known as the father of science fiction.

The Voyage to the Moon, *by Cyrano de Bergerac. Long before Jules Verne, French writer Cyrano de Bergerac imagined a voyage to the Moon in something reminiscent of an outhouse. Well, at least astronauts would have had ready access to the facilities.*

Before writing a single word, Verne met with an astronomer and presented the challenge: to send three astronauts to the moon and bring them back again within a reasonable amount of time. The astronomer helped Verne work out trajectories, velocities, vehicle size and shape—even g-forces on takeoff. Absolutely nobody else had been so serious about designing what amounted to a paper rocket.

The result of Verne's hard work is almost scary. The *Columbiad* looks strangely like *Apollo 11*'s command module—short, squat, and conical. It was launched from Florida, carried three astronauts into lunar orbit, and made the trip in three days. Even more striking is *Columbiad*'s return to Earth; it splashed down in the Pacific!

So why, you may be wondering, did it take us almost a full century before we actually managed to do it for real?

Well, contrary to what Verne, H. G. Wells, and Captain Kirk have led us all to believe, space travel is not nearly as easy as it looks.

It was the early 1900s and a young Robert Goddard, raised on the stories of H. G. Wells, was building little rockets in his backyard. His neighbors, however, were far from delighted.

Goddard fed the gunpowder into the narrow chamber and stepped back. He hoped the explosion wouldn't be too loud.

It was deafening.

All the way down the entire block, it seemed, windows shot open and angry heads popped out like jack-in-the-boxes. There was a good deal of shouting, nearly all of which Goddard ignored. He had more important things to think about.

Goddard stared at the smoldering rocket remains on the grass. Another failure. But Goddard's fertile mind continued to sift through a hundred different ideas. Hmm . . . Maybe gunpowder wasn't the right kind of fuel after all. . . .

Goddard rubbed his chin. The stuff was just a little too explosive, too unpredictable. . . .

Hmm . . . maybe . . .

And slowly, faintly, a light began to burn behind Goddard's clear eyes.

By 1926 hemlines had risen to shocking heights. Cars were everywhere, and Charles Lindbergh was toying with the idea of crossing the Atlantic in (of all things) an airplane! As for Goddard, he was still in his backyard, but he was no longer fiddling around with gunpowder rockets. He had come up with a new design, something quite spectacular, he thought, and he could hardly wait to get it on the launch pad.

After a brief ceremony during which Goddard's new wife took a picture of her husband the inventor, Goddard launched the world's first liquid-fueled rocket. Driven by a mixture of gasoline and liquid oxygen, the little four-foot-tall rocket headed upward with a ferocious roar.

Goddard's neighbors may have thought they were sharing their block with a nut, but when the Smithsonian Institution found out what Goddard was doing up there in Massachusetts, they promptly gave him a few thousand dollars to continue his research. While a few thousand dollars was hardly a fortune, it would at least keep Goddard in metal tubes and chemicals. So for the next three years, the father of it all tinkered and fiddled until in July 1929 he launched a wow of a rocket. It was big and fast and carried a small payload. But the roar was positively ear-shattering, and this time Goddard's neighbors decided they'd had quite enough of the rocket man's shenanigans. They called the police.

Goddard might have been down. He might have been the laughingstock of Auburn, Massachusetts, but it was just about at this point that he suddenly found himself blessed with a guardian angel: the exceedingly rich and generous Daniel Guggenheim. Guggenheim learned of Goddard's experiments from Charles Lindbergh, who had visited Goddard and seen the fledgling rockets. Lindbergh had been so impressed, he'd persuaded Guggenheim to cough up some hard cash so the world could get on with the business of traveling into space. Guggenheim's grant turned out to be a

Goddard poses in the snow beside his liquid oxygen/gasoline rocket. The first of its kind, Goddard's rocket became the early prototype for the mighty Saturn V.

ESTHER C. GODDARD PHOTO, COURTESY AIP, NEILS BOHR LIBRARY

rather hefty fifty thousand dollars, which Goddard used to set up his rocket shop in Roswell, New Mexico. Nobody to complain about the noise out there.

By 1935, Goddard had developed some very impressive stuff. His vehicles were hitting speeds in excess of five hundred miles an hour and climbing almost a mile and a half through the atmosphere. They even had gyroscopes to keep them on a straight course.

Now, you would think with success like this, the government would have stepped in, jammed thousand-dollar bills into Goddard's pockets, and told him to keep building. But the government barely noticed the big doings in Roswell. True, the higher-ups in Washington did contact Goddard once World War II broke out, but it sure wasn't because President Roosevelt wanted to be an astronaut. Goddard was commissioned to design small rockets to help launch navy planes. So by pretty much ignoring Robert Goddard and what would eventually become the prototype for the *Saturn V* rocket, the United States got caught with its pants down when Russia quietly launched the world's first orbiting satellite. The year was 1957, and the little traveler was named *Sputnik*. To say the politicians in Washington panicked would be putting it mildly.

It hardly mattered that *Sputnik* weighed all of 184 pounds or that it was destined to transmit messages to Earth for just three weeks. Too unsophisticated to maintain its orbit, the little globular craft would fall from the sky on its three-month birthday and burn to a crisp on the way home. Its launch vehicle had been nothing more than an intercontinental ballistic missile, fondly referred to as Old Number Seven. High-tech intergalactic rocketry this was not, but it certainly shook up the crowd in Washington.

Desperate to save face, the United States answered the Russians in kind and on January 31, 1958, launched *Explorer 1.* It rose spectacularly on a pillar of flame from a single-stage Jupiter C rocket, which was really just another modified intermediate-range ballistic missile. For the American public who had not even seen this sort of thing on TV's "Captain Video," the event was truly out of this world, but for the rocket scientists, it was the beginning of the nightmare. No matter how promising Goddard had made the liquid-fueled rocket look, it turned out to be big and clumsy and nothing but trouble.

It all began fabulously enough. The rockets stood tall and proud upon the launchpads at Cape Canaveral. We oohed and aahed and commented on how really *big* they were. That was their problem.

On launch days we gathered in front of our TVs with the big screens and counted down with the scientists who stood nervously in the launch bunkers. *Five . . . four . . . three . . . two . . . one . . . ignition!*

Then there was a breath as the rocket gathered all its strength for the great and strenuous climb. Flames and white billowing steam erupted from the silver exhaust cones, and the roar advanced like the thunder of a moving army.

"Go-go-go-go-go!" we shouted, urging the outer space ship along on its date with destiny. We clapped. We cheered. We pointed, swelling with pride for our country, with the joy of just being alive to witness this wondrous event.

And then in slow motion, almost, the rockets leaned and crashed to the ground, exploding in a heartbreak of ruin. Some managed to scramble their way upward a little before tilting and then arcing back down to Earth, where their fuel tanks burst and caught fire in front of 150 million dejected American faces.

They tried again. Always they tried again, but the rockets

were too big and heavy for the meager thrust we had given them. Gravity overpowered the engines and the exhaust velocity, and the rockets could not escape. The months of failures hung like a velvet drape. Outer space seemed farther away than ever.

Now, it was right around this time that a major cereal manufacturer taught many of us the naked truth about rocket propulsion. Within specially marked boxes of our very favorite breakfast food was the classic of all cereal freebies—a navy frogman, brightly colored and made of plastic. The frogman stood on a small chamber into which you poured baking powder. That was his "fuel." In a hurried ceremony, you stood the frogman on the edge of the bathtub, yelled "Dive!" or some reasonable facsimile, and had him plunge into the tepid waters. The baking powder reacted with the water and produced carbon dioxide gas and calcium acid

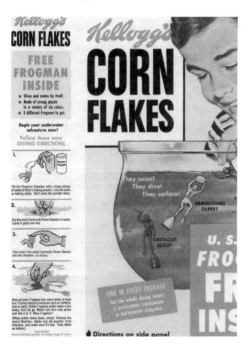

The Kellogg Company taught all of us about rocket propulsion way back in the 1950s with its fabulous navy frogman giveaway.

COURTESY KELLOGG COMPANY

phosphate, which provided what a rocket scientist would call thrust, and *zip! zip! zip!* the frogman shot around the tub.

Spaceships, of course, cannot run on baking powder and water, but like the frogman, they operate according to the same physical laws—namely those dreamed up by Sir Isaac Newton over three hundred years ago. Newton's three laws of motion are simple and elegant and explain how things can be made to go from one place to another—plastic frogmen and the *Saturn V* included.

The first problem that rocket scientists face is described, appropriately enough, by Newton's first law, which says that objects don't like to be moved. This is called inertia.* (Actually, Galileo, who was known to toss things out of the top floor window of the Leaning Tower of Pisa, thought of inertia first, but Newton turned it into a package deal.)

Inertia is everywhere. Clyde Leadfoot's '69 Gran Fury has carburetor trouble on the entrance ramp to the expressway. Muttering under his breath, Clyde goes nuts trying to restart his car, but it won't kick in. "Hey!" yells an irate driver who has pulled up behind Clyde. "Get that heap outta here!"

Muttering louder now, Clyde shifts the Fury into neutral, gets out of the car, closes the door, braces himself against the rear bumper, and proceeds to push. But Clyde is more talk than muscle, and he cannot even budge the Fury. The problem is the car's inertia and Newton's first law of motion: Objects at rest tend to remain at rest.

You will smirk and say, "Well, of course, Clyde can't move the car. The thing weighs a couple of tons."

Exactly. So now try to imagine how hard it is to get a rocket moving from a dead stop.

But we don't push rockets. Rockets move through space a

---

*You probably don't need the help, but it's here anyway: IN **ER** SHUH.

lot like the little baking-powder frogman in the bathtub, and that is strictly according to Newton's third law of motion. Newton's third law states that "every action produces an equal and opposite reaction." So picture a rocket on the launchpad. At the word, *"Ignition!"* a tremendous roar explodes from the rocket's engines, and a powerful blast of flame, gases, and other kinds of exhaust material shoots out of the tail. This exhaust material is moving at a very fast speed *downward,** and, as Newton promised, the rocket begins to inch *upward.* Material leaves the rocket in one direction, and, *voilà!* the rocket moves in the opposite direction!

But just hold it a minute. Something's not quite right, here. Maybe those exhaust materials are streaming out of the rocket at a furious speed. But what's the story with that rocket? Is it tearing upward at the same rate of speed, the way Newton said? Does its upward velocity match the downward velocity of its exhaust?

Absolutely not! E-v-e-r so s-l-o-w-l-y the rocket begins its ascent, inching along, gradually going a little bit faster, then a little bit more. . . .

And meanwhile those engines are really roaring, and the exhaust materials are racing out the tail end!

. . . and the rocket is s-l-o-w-l-y accelerating, s-l-o-w-l-y increasing its speed . . .

Hey! You call this "equal and opposite"?

It should be pointed out that Newton's laws (in case you were thinking that Newton might be at fault) are absolutely correct. They have been proved countless times. So we must be overlooking something very important about this launch business, something we haven't taken into consideration.

---

*The speed at which exhaust material leaves the rocket is called the exhaust velocity. A snappy exhaust velocity is essential for getting rockets off the ground and into space.

Inertia, maybe?

Clyde's biggest challenge in getting his car onto the shoulder of the expressway is setting it in motion from a dead stop. Because of its tremendous weight, moving it that first eighth of an inch will require enormous energy. But Clyde should just be glad he doesn't have to move a rocket because not only do we have to overcome inertia, we have the extra added attraction of gravity.*

Earth, as you know if you have ever dropped something on your foot, is a very attractive planet. This attraction is called gravity, from the Latin word *gravis* meaning "heavy." The scientific world was sure that Newton had the concept of gravity all sewn up until Einstein came along. Originally, gravity was thought to be a "pull." This somewhat mysterious "pull of gravity" kept the planets in their orbits and all kinds of things stuck to the Earth. Einstein, however, suggested that gravity was a phenomenon of space itself.

Try to imagine a gigantic rubber sheet or the fabric on a trampoline. This, said Einstein, is space. Now, into space we will place a few planets and stars, asteroids, dust, and all that sort of thing. This would be like putting a bowling ball, a couple of baseballs, and some marbles on the rubber sheet. What happens? Well, according to Einstein, planets as well as bowling balls all make dents in the fabric, and the heavier, or more massive, the object, the deeper the dent. So in Einstein's universe, gravity is not a force but a kind of depression in space caused by the presence of objects. Whenever something such as a comet gets close to a star's gravity well, it starts to roll downward toward the star.

Absolutely everything that exists in the universe creates a

---

*No gravity for Clyde. He is not trying to get his car off the Earth. All he wants to do is push it across the Earth's surface.

gravitational field—from molecules to planets—and the objects with the greatest amount of mass naturally create the strongest gravitational attraction. While the Earth is far from the most massive planet in the solar system, it is not a lightweight either, so its gravitational field is rather respectable. That makes it hard for the rocket scientists to launch heavy things from the surface. The rocket has to "climb" up out of Earth's gravity well, and to do this, the rocket needs a lot of power. Scientists call this power *thrust*. Sufficient thrust is what so many of those early rockets didn't have. The engines kicked in; the rocket wobbled, but it couldn't rise. There just wasn't enough downward force to overcome the massive weight of the craft because of Earth's gravitational attraction for it.

So does the "equal and opposite" law work? Yes, absolutely, but we've got to get the rocket out of the clutches of gravity first.

As the mighty *Saturn V* stood on the launchpad waiting to carry *Apollo 11* to the moon, the TV commentators waxed poetic about the F-1 engines on the first stage. There were five, each capable of delivering an awesome 1.5 million pounds of thrust. Five J-2 engines were mounted on the second stage, and one was on the third. But it was the F-1s that were solely responsible for actually lifting the entire spacecraft—all 6 million pounds of it—off the Earth.

In just two and a half minutes, those five engines sucked up over half a million gallons of refined kerosene and liquid oxygen (LOX) just to move the rocket a measly 38 miles through the atmosphere. When the empty fuel tanks dropped away, the *Saturn V* was only going some 6,100 miles an hour. While Clyde Leadfoot would probably trade his entire collection of vintage *Hot Rod* magazines to be able to do 6,100 miles an hour, this speed would not have put *Apollo 11* much of anywhere.

SATURN SA-6 VEHICLE

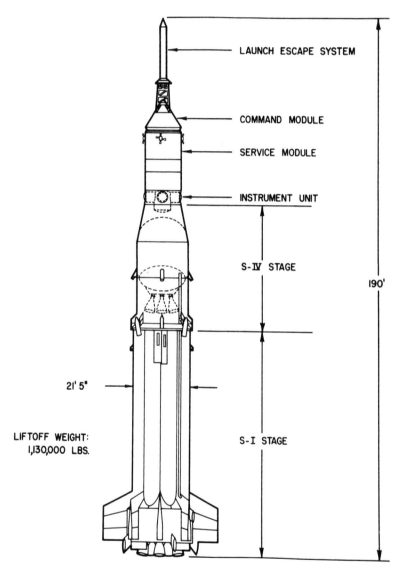

*S*imilar to the SA-6, the Saturn V launch vehicle had little room for anything except fuel and oxidant tanks. Its liftoff weight was more than 1 million pounds.

NASA

Remember gravity? Well, in order to break free of Earth's gravitational hold, a rocket needs a running start. This running start is called *escape velocity* because, quite logically, the rocket is trying to escape the planet's clutches. A rocket that doesn't make escape velocity will do one of two things: go into orbit, or, if it is really poking along, nosedive back to Earth.

Escape velocity depends on the strength of an object's gravitational field. The stronger the gravity, the higher the escape velocity has to be. Earth's escape velocity is 7 miles a second, or 25,200 miles an hour. Sounds like quite a challenge, but if you could land on the sun, you'd have to crank up your rocket to about 383 miles a second—well over 1,000,000 miles an hour!—to get away.

Now, when we last left *Saturn V* it was chugging along at 6,100 miles an hour, and 6,100 miles an hour is not anywhere near escape velocity. (Ironically, a speed of 6,100 miles an hour will get us to the moon in about a day and a half, but it won't get us off the Earth.) Since there was no more fuel in the first stage (it had been used up in the time it takes to watch three commercials on television), the NASA engineers had to attach a second stage. This one had an easier job since the spacecraft was already moving, but even with five more fuel-guzzling engines and better than 350,000 gallons of LOX and liquid hydrogen, final speed six minutes later when the gas tank was empty was still wide of the mark: 15,300 miles an hour.

So the engineers slapped on a third stage with an 83,000-gallon tank and a single engine. The fuel was gone from this stage in two minutes, adding another 2,100 miles an hour to the craft's speed.

Total velocity now: 17,400 miles an hour

Target velocity for escape: 25,200 miles an hour

Some tough job this was turning out to be! Three gigantic fuel tanks and a total of *eleven* engines, and *Apollo* still wasn't in outer space. What was the big problem?

The problem, in a word, was the *fuel*. The fuel drove the engineers nuts. It was inefficient. It was heavy. And its exhaust velocity wasn't so great either. For all their high-tech sound, liquid rocket propellants are not much better than the super premium gasoline that Clyde Leadfoot puts into his Fury. First, in order for it to work, liquid rocket fuel must undergo combustion, just like gasoline. When gasoline is fired into the cylinders of a car it mixes with air, but in space there is no air, so the rocket has to carry a substitute. It's not air, exactly, but something called an *oxidant* (from the word *oxygen*). The oxidant for the *Saturn V* was in the form of a liquid—liquid oxygen—and the stuff weighs a ton—165 tons, actually, in the first stage alone.

Now, mind you, this liquid oxygen is not fuel. In the first stage of the *Saturn V*, kerosene was the fuel; the LOX only went along to provide oxygen to burn the kerosene to provide the needed exhaust velocity to move the rocket. Because of this combustion thing, the *Saturn V* had to carry a few million extra pounds! These were millions of pounds that had to be lifted off the Earth, millions of pounds that forced the engineers to keep slapping on more and more heavy fuel tanks. And the more tanks we had to lift, the more fuel we needed to help lift them!

Another problem with liquid fuels is their low exhaust velocity, because they must be coupled with traditional engines, which can't expel the waste products very fast. So when Newton's "equal and opposite" law goes into effect, the absolute top speed of the rocket is, maybe, 30,000 miles an hour.

But is this really so bad? Thirty thousand miles an hour sounds awfully fast. If we ignore the time it takes to accelerate the ship and then slow it down again, 30,000 miles an hour could get us to the moon in eight hours. It could get us to Mars in about two months.

But at the modest speed of 30,000 miles an hour, a one-way trip to the nearest star, Proxima Centauri, would take roughly 95,000 years. That is running on the liquid fuel we use today, launched from the surface of the Earth in something closely resembling the *Saturn V/Apollo* setup.

No, we do not have space travel.

"Warp speed, Mr. Sulu."

Sorry. We can't.

Because in real life, it's not as easy as it looks. ★

CHAPTER 2

★

Bombs Away!

*T*he government called it the Manhattan Project. It sounded perfectly harmless. It was supposed to. Everything had been classified Top Secret and carefully hidden behind colorful, almost cartoonish code names: Fat Man, Little Boy, the Dragon, Thin Man. Quietly and without fanfare, the government boys assembled the team— engineers, chemists, physicists, mathematicians—each with his or her own specialty, each absolutely vital to the success of the project: building an atomic bomb.

One after the other, the scientists were brought to a high mesa in northern New Mexico just outside Santa Fe. It was beautiful there, as only the Southwest can be, gently forested and dotted with ancient Indian cliff dwellings. The town was called Los Alamos, "the poplars," but for six days a week, nobody noticed. That's when they worked on the bomb.

The months crawled along as the scientists calculated the hydrodynamics and tested the explosive lenses. They assembled the plutonium and uranium. They built the casings and the triggering mechanism. Overhead, the sun climbed toward the mesas, marking the time.

By July 1945 the scientists had moved downstate. The flat, open desert would provide a good test site. When the thing went up, it would probably be big, and the boys in the government wanted to hide the blast as best they could. So they chose a vast, sparsely populated area not far from the Mexican border. It was known as Alamogordo.

The engineers erected a tall steel tower among the scrub and cactuses. Dry winds blew through the open framework, and at night if you stood under it, you could see a perfect sky dotted with icy white stars. But then they fitted the initiator—the device that starts the chain reaction—into the core and mounted the whole assembly in a heavy outer casing. They drove it out to the desert and lowered it into place. And then they left, and the tower wasn't just a tower anymore. It was ground zero.

July 16, 1945. Monday. The scientists and the government boys gathered in the bunkers, and by the dawn's early light they tested the bomb. They knew what they would see, but they didn't really know. They knew the math and they understood the physics—20 billion individual fission reactions every second, each one releasing a small bit of energy and adding up to a power never before seen on Earth.

"If only I had known," said Albert Einstein woefully, "I should have become a watchmaker."

They counted down to zero as the sun was beginning to rise, and then the desert exploded. The flash of light was painfully, almost impossibly bright. In a six-thousandth of a second, the light had formed itself into a swelling ball of gas.

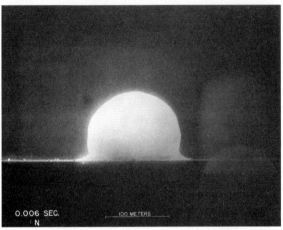

0.006 SEC.
N

100 METERS

0.016 SEC.
N

100 METERS

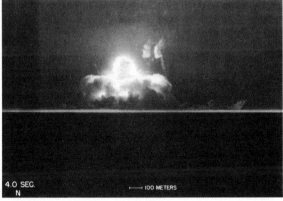

The astonishing power of nuclear fission can be seen in the atomic explosion at the Alamogordo, New Mexico, test site in the 1940s.

LOS ALAMOS NATIONAL LABORATORY

Two seconds later the characteristic mushroom stem had grown visible, and by four seconds, the death cloud was spilling its radioactive contents into the warm, clean air over Alamogordo.

The sound from the explosion ebbed slowly away, but the cloud continued to expand. Air currents scattered the test bomb cloud until there was nothing left but a plutonium echo. Sometime later, project director Robert Oppenheimer ventured out into the desert to see what the bomb had done at ground zero. The Geiger counters clicked threateningly. The tower, of course, was gone. All that remained were a few charred and twisted reinforcing rods from the concrete footings. The enormous heat generated by the bomb had fused the sand into green glass, and a massive radioactive crater was easily visible from the air.

Human beings had released the energy from within the atom. Now they could go to the stars.

It was the Greek philosopher Democritus (born sometime around 460 B.C.) who first suggested the basic idea of the atom. He proposed that matter was made of tiny bits, far too tiny to be seen with the naked eye, but essential to the structure of everything—from ants to planets. Democritus was certainly on the right track, although he thought the atom—which means, "not able to be divided"—was as small as it got.

Atomic theory went pretty much nowhere for some two thousand years, mainly because Aristotle—the philosopher with the most clout in those early days—decided Democritus had flipped his wig with all that silly talk about atoms. "Preposterous!" was Aristotle's opinion, and because nobody wanted to buck the great Aristotle, Democritus's atoms died without further ado.

It wasn't until the beginning of the 1800s that English chemist John Dalton reintroduced the concept of the atom. But after a somewhat tricky experiment, Dalton concluded that the atom was not the end of the line; it was almost certainly made of even smaller particles.

By the 1830s, Michael Faraday, another English scientist, had discovered that atoms are electrically charged. Some parts of the atom, said Faraday, carry a positive charge, and some, a negative charge. So the atom is really made of more than one piece, but because opposite charges attract each other, all the pieces remain firmly stuck together.

Faraday didn't know what this electrically charged atom might look like, but his colleague, Sir Joseph John Thomson, certainly thought he did. After Thomson found the electron in 1897, he concluded that an atom was some kind of a positively charged ball with negatively charged electrons firmly imbedded in it, reminiscent of a scoop of chocolate chip ice cream.

Today scientists describe the atom as looking more like a miniature solar system. In the center of the atom sits the nucleus with most of the atom's mass (such as it is). Far from the nucleus—in atomic terms—are the electrons, whirling madly on their axes* as they race around the nucleus in assigned orbits, called *shells.*

Faraday was correct when he suggested that the atom's opposite charges work like a kind of glue keeping the negative electrons close to the positively charged nucleus. But that's not nearly the end of the story. Cleverly concealed within the nucleus of the atom is yet another kind of particle—the neutron—although for years, nobody had even the slightest

---

*Despite what this looks like, we are not talking about more than one ax. This *axes* is plural for *axis.*

idea the thing existed. In fact, when Australian physicist Ernest Rutherford nailed the proton in 1911, he completely missed the neutron. Here's why.

In the tiny, tiny world of atomic physics, scientists don't see things as much as they infer that things exist. So Rutherford never actually looked the proton in the eye. Instead, he performed an experiment in which he shot a small, positively charged particle, called an *alpha particle,* at what amounted to a big bundle of atoms. The object was to learn how the alpha particle would negotiate its way through all the force fields within the atoms. Since an alpha particle has a positive charge, it would be attracted to anything with a negative charge (the electrons), and be repelled, or pushed away, by anything with a positive charge.

Rutherford figured that some of the alpha particles would enter the bundle of atoms and be absorbed, attracted by the negatively charged electrons, and that is indeed what happened. But to Rutherford's surprise and delight, quite a few of the alpha particles shot through the bundle of atoms and were deflected. They went in straight and came out to the left somewhere, or to the right, as if something had knocked them off course. And something had: a particle with a positive charge—the proton. What a clever experiment! Except it wasn't clever enough to catch the neutron.

The nucleus of an atom is packed very tightly with protons and neutrons, rather like a cluster of grapes. So it stands to reason that an alpha particle could hardly fail to avoid all those neutrons, and, of course, it didn't. It's just that nothing happened to the alpha particles when they encountered the neutrons. Nothing could happen. Neutrons are neutral, and without an electromagnetic charge, they couldn't affect the path of the alpha particles.

The neutrons turned out to be very slippery customers

and weren't detected until 1932, more than twenty years after Rutherford found the proton. It had been quite a hunt, but at last science had a fairly accurate picture of the atom: a swirling cloud of negatively charged electrons encircling a nucleus that consists (usually) of an equal number of protons and neutrons. The positively charged nucleus attracts the negatively charged electrons, and life on the atomic level is very merry.

Except for one little problem. If only opposite charges attract, what's keeping the neutrons and protons in the nucleus stuck together?

This seemingly innocent little question is actually a whopper of the first magnitude. Its answer is the essence of atomic fission. It is the reason why the scientists and the boys from Washington were able to blow a large hole in the desert near Alamogordo. And it is the reason why the rocket engineers could begin to design serious starships.

The particles in the nucleus are held together by what scientists call the strong force, and they are not kidding. This is the monster. It is really a kind of nuclear Super Glue, 100,000,000,000,000,000,000,000,000,000,000,000,000 times stronger than gravity. Gravity, you will recall, keeps the moon close to the Earth, the planets close to the sun, and the sun within the galaxy. But it is the force binding the particles in a tiny atomic nucleus that is absolutely the strongest in nature.*

Just after the turn of the twentieth century, Albert Einstein had predicted that a little bit of matter would pack quite a wallop if it were ever converted into pure energy. A single pound of helium—the second lightest element in the uni-

---

*But if there's a strong force, you may be thinking, why do we need gravity? Well, unfortunately—or fortunately, depending on how you look at it—the strong force only works for extremely short distances.

verse—could produce enough energy to power a ten-watt light bulb for a hundred million years.*

Is this a possible power source for an interstellar ship? You bet! The only problem is, we haven't really figured out a good way to convert even one atom into pure energy without any leftovers.† But Einstein's theories about mass and energy also show that there is a fair amount of oomph locked within the nucleus of the atom. So if we could somehow break up the nucleus, we would release the energy. This, however, was easier said than done.

To split the nucleus of the atom, scientists knew they would need some sort of bullet. It would have to be a high-speed particle that could get past the swirling cloud of electrons and then successfully crash into the tightly packed group of protons and neutrons. A particle with a negative charge was no good because it would never get past the negative electrons, and the heavier the element, the more electrons there are! Positive particles—protons, for instance—weren't any better. Even if they could slip in between the electrons, they'd be repelled by the positively charged nucleus. So the best atom-smashing bullet is a particle with no charge at all—a neutron.

The process of breaking up atomic nuclei (plural of nucleus) is called *nuclear fission*, from the Latin word *findere*, meaning, "to split."‡ In nuclear fission, a small, high-speed atomic particle is shot at the nucleus of a "heavy" atom, one

---

*If the dinosaurs had discovered how to completely convert mass into energy, and if they had used the energy to light a little night light just before they became extinct, the bulb would still be burning today.

†We have taken a shot at it, though, and you will find our explosion attempts in Chapter 6.

‡In the next chapter you will encounter fusion, a totally different process for producing energy. To avoid confusion, think of splitting the two s's in fission.

---

that has a large number of protons and neutrons. Since the bombarding particle is neutral, it can easily slip into the nucleus, but once inside it is detected by the other particles as an intruder.

Suddenly there is panic on the atomic level as the nucleus struggles with this new and decidedly unfavorable development. But that is just exactly what the scientists want, because when a nucleus is invaded it has a little nervous breakdown and splits apart. And when the nucleus splits, the strong force is broken, and energy is released.

The energy from one nucleus is hardly enough to power a starship, so the object is to get a chain reaction going.* When the nucleus divides, it releases neutrons—naturally, since there are neutrons in the nucleus. These neutrons then become bullets that smash into adjoining nuclei. The smashed nuclei release still more neutron bullets, and so on, and so on, and so on. Since the whole process occurs in the tiniest fraction of a second, a walloping amount of energy is produced, as the explosion of the atomic bomb at Hiroshima proved.

The fission reactions occur so fast that in one second there are 20 billion of them. Furthermore, each reaction yields twice as much energy as the one before it. So if the first nucleus breakup releases 200 million electron volts of energy, the second yields 400 million; the third, 800 million, the fourth, one billion six hundred million (1,600,000,000); the fifth, more than 3 billion electron volts, doubling at an astonishing rate. In less than an eye blink (1/25th of a second), we can fission a pound of uranium 235 providing enough energy to keep a 100-watt light bulb burning for 15,000 years, or 15,000

---

*Simple example of a chain reaction: two thousand dominoes all lined up. The last domino loses its balance and falls against the one next to it. . . .

100-watt light bulbs burning for one year. No wonder nuclear energy seems so attractive to power companies.

A full fourteen years before *Apollo* was launched, the United States decided to take a shot at developing nuclear rockets, so in 1955 the Rover Project was born. Rover fell within the joint jurisdiction of the Atomic Energy Commission (AEC) and the air force, and was kept ultrasecret. The proposed rocket would contain an actual nuclear reactor with radioactive uranium 235 as fuel, although the uranium would not be expelled from the rocket. Instead, it would be used to heat the liquid hydrogen that would serve as the propellant.

In the Rover prototype, the liquid hydrogen would pass through the reactor along enclosed channels. There, the tremendous temperatures generated by the fission reactions would heat the hydrogen to many thousands of degrees. The hydrogen would then be expelled from the rocket nozzles to provide the thrust.

Actually, this system is strikingly similar to the good old jet engine/liquid fuel setup that NASA has been clinging to for so many decades. Liquid hydrogen is still being used, but because a nuclear reactor replaces the internal combustion engine, there is no need to carry an oxidant like liquid oxygen. (The oxidant, remember, substitutes for the air so that combustion can take place.) The benefit of this is pretty obvious. Without the burden of an oxidant, there's no need to carry so many fuel tanks, and the ship becomes much lighter. Also, uranium fission produces tremendous heat, so when the hydrogen leaves the craft, it is a lot hotter, and moving a lot faster, than it would be if it were run through a standard F-1 or J-2 engine. This allows the rocket to achieve a higher speed. But is it high enough? Is the nuclear system really any better?

By 1960, NASA and the government were very enthusiastic about nuclear propulsion systems. They had already selected a site in the Nevada desert for testing the rocket prototypes. The first reactor engine had gone through its paces the year before, but because it was only a ground-based test (no flying), the engine was named Kiwi A, after the large, flight-

Kiwi A could have been the rocket engine of the future, but it never got off the ground.

less bird of New Zealand. Kiwi A performed beautifully, just as the engineers had hoped, so everyone was encouraged to try for a bigger and more powerful Kiwi B.

After much tinkering and many design adjustments, the engineers at last produced what they felt was an efficient nuclear reactor that would actually work when it was plunked into a rocket. The first test flight was planned for 1968, but as the time grew closer, prospects began to look worse and worse for NASA and Rover. Due, probably, to the huge expenses of the Vietnam War, NASA's budget was chopped to pieces. Aptly named Kiwi B never got off the ground.

Meanwhile, in Los Alamos, New Mexico, Dr. Stanislaw Ulam and his team were trying to figure out how to shrink atomic bombs for the government.* The plan was to make the bombs more portable, less devastating, and easier to drop so they could be used in large construction projects, such as building dams. Ulam, however, had something a lot more fun in mind.

In 1891 a German inventor named Hermann Gainswindt had proposed tossing bombs out the tail end of a rocket to provide thrust. The power generated as the bombs exploded, said Gainswindt, would boost the craft to rather impressive speeds and make space travel a reality. This was quite an idea considering the Wright brothers had not yet flown at Kitty Hawk. Gainswindt was a good half century before Alamogordo and atomic energy, so it is certain that he did not have nuclear bombs in mind. But Dr. Ulam did.

Ulam took the basic concept from Gainswindt and updated it to fit into the atomic age. He called his ship design a *nuclear*

---

*In case you are wondering why the government is always involved in everything, it's because nobody else really has the big money necessary to fund this kind of research. Recently, however, private companies have started to consider partnerships in space technology.

pulse rocket since each thermonuclear explosion would produce a kickback, or a pulse, directly behind the ship. Ulam guessed that these pulses would be felt inside the ship, so he proposed fitting the craft with shock absorbers to smooth out the ride.

The government—particularly the Department of Defense—took a fancy to Ulam's rocket idea and set Ulam up in business under the name Project Orion. So in the 1950s, while Howdy Doody was asking kids what time it was, the U.S. government had, not one, but *two* nuclear rocket projects going on in the southwestern desert.

The design that eventually won Ulam a vote of confidence from the government was a 12-ton spacecraft that could carry up to 100 small nuclear bombs. The bombs would be shot like BBs from the aft part of the ship one each second, providing a continuous, pulsing stream. At the same time, individual packets of solid propellant would be fired in the direction of the nuclear explosions. The enormous temperatures generated when the bombs exploded would heat the propellant, which would in turn accelerate the ship. While Ulam's idea was far too rough and unfinished to really work, it was good enough to earn a series of patents for its basic blueprint, and in 1958 Ulam got started on Orion.

The final design looked like something out of an episode of "Flash Gordon." The overwhelming effect was one of smooth curves and shiny steel, of perfect geometric shapes that seemed almost to snap together like a set of metallic Lego blocks. The crew module, as with nearly all the ships that were to follow, sat in the extreme fore section, with the sleeping accommodations, recreational facilities, and galley housed in a large cubicle structure behind the bridge.

Next came the cluster of cylinders that held the propellant, and in back of that, the pulse unit delivery system. In the stern of the ship was the massive pusher plate off which the nuclear explosions would rebound, looking, as its name suggests, like a giant dinner plate. Cushioning came from the primary shock absorber fitted to the pusher plate and an array of long, spidery secondary shock absorbers that attached to the pulse unit. Even today, almost half a century after Orion was conceived, the craft still seems mildly futuristic, probably due to the strange configuration of the shock absorbers and pusher plate. But even Flash Gordon couldn't have imagined the scene as Orion cruised the galaxy.

With no air to carry the sound waves, the bombs would explode in total silence half a ship's length away. Between the gleaming bullet-shaped craft and the bursts of white light there would be nothing but spaceblack dotted by chips of silver stars. The gases from the blasts would expand outward like smoke rings, perfect for a time, but then stretching and slowly falling apart. Once target speed was achieved, the reactor would be shut down, and Orion would glide on to its destination, unheard and unseen, across the dark light-years.* Truly, Orion was a beauty, but it was also a beast.

The fissioning of uranium 235 could provide enough energy to get a starship of modest size up to over 8,000 miles a second, or better than 28 million miles an hour. This would put a crew on Pluto in about a week, not counting acceleration and deceleration. That's certainly beautiful, but not so beautiful is the fact that Pluto lies a mere 3 billion miles away. The nearest star—which may or may not have planets on which to land—is more than four light-years away. A one-way trip in an Orion-type rocket would take over a century,

---

*A light-year is the distance light can travel in one year, doing a steady 186,282 miles per second. It is roughly 6 trillion miles.

certainly not very feasible if you want everybody to get there while they are still alive.

But Orion was doomed to failure from the very beginning, from the moment the uranium was loaded onto the ship. Atomic fission produces deadly radioactive fallout. This means that when an atomic nucleus splits, rather hideous particles and rays emerge. Science has known about these by-products for quite some time, and it was Ernest Rutherford back in the 1930s who gave them all names. He called them alpha and beta particles and gamma rays.

Naturally, Ulam had foreseen the problem of uranium's "dirty" by-products and designed Orion with heavy shielding for the crew and instruments. But if Orion were launched from Earth everyone on the ground would still be at high risk. Alpha and beta particles and gamma radiation all have penetrating ability; that is, they can go through things. Alpha particles (which consist of two protons and two neutrons) do not have much energy and can easily be stopped. Beta particles are escaped electrons moving at high speed, but they can be deflected by a magnetic field. It's the gamma rays that are the problem.

Gamma rays are very energetic and can penetrate all kinds of materials, not least of which is living cells.* Extremely thick lead shielding will stop gamma radiation, but that won't help anybody standing on the ground when a nuclear-powered rocket is launched. So the only sensible place to launch such a vehicle is from space. And that was not something we were prepared to do in the 1950s. We can't even do it now.

---

*The French chemist Marie Curie developed leukemia as a result of her experiments with radioactive substances, primarily radium. In 1935, she was awarded the Nobel Prize for chemistry posthumously; she had died of cancer the year before. Gamma rays are nasty stuff.

The beginning of the end for Orion came in 1963 when the U.S.S.R., the United States, and Great Britain signed the Nuclear Test Ban Treaty. Three and a half years later, the death knell sounded throughout NASA when the Outer Space Treaty banned the introduction of nuclear weapons into space. Orion, of course, was not carrying nuclear weapons per se, but it was going to be loaded down with fissionable uranium, and a bomb by any other name is still very much a bomb.

Orion was never built, although a nuclear pulse engine was. Engineers tested it in secret on the ground in a protected environment, and then shut it down. It had worked, but it was never to work again, and much of what went on out

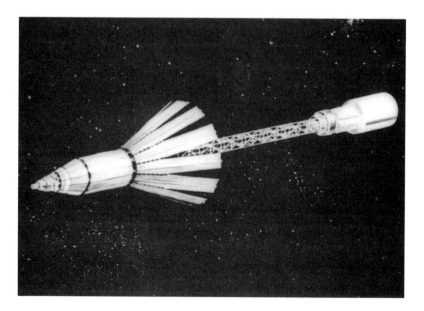

This experimental nuclear-powered ship is part of NASA's Project Pathfinder. Designed as a short-range craft, it will probably never see deep space. Its modest goal is merely to carry voyagers to Mars.
NASA

there in the desert is still shrouded in government secrecy.

But perhaps it's just as well. When all was said and done, everyone had to admit that in addition to being a radioactive polluter of the first order, the nuclear pulse rocket could not be made very efficient. In the Orion design, much of the energy from the explosions was allowed to escape into space, so the top speed for such a craft would never have been enough to get us to the stars.

Quietly, almost ceremonially, Orion's folder was sealed, stamped CLASSIFIED, and made to disappear as only the government knows how to do. And a couple of years later, when we heard the faraway voice of *Apollo 11* astronaut Neil Armstrong say, "That's one small step for a man, one giant leap for mankind," as he bounced out onto the lunar surface, we never knew how true it was. ★

CHAPTER 3

★

Hot Stuff

*I*n 1938 physicist Hans Bethe announced that he had at last figured out why the sun is so hot. This question had been plaguing scientists for a very long time, and through the years they had come up with some pretty fanciful ideas. The earliest peoples knew only about basic combustion, so they naturally assumed that the sun was just one big bonfire. But it soon began to dawn on the scientists and philosophers that simple burning was not going to do it. How old was the Earth? they asked themselves. Awfully old. Has the sun been shining the entire time? Seems that way. Some fire, that must be, to keep going like that for what, at current estimates, is about 8 billion years.

The first clue that the sun was using some exotic heat-generating process came just around the turn of the century. English astronomer Arthur Eddington had concluded that the sun had to be made of some light material—not rocks and carbon compounds, but gas. New techniques had allowed scientists to measure the densities of the Earth and sun, and the sun unquestionably came out the loser. If a cup of Earth and a cup of sun could be put on a scale, the cup of sun would weigh much less. Conclusion: The sun is a giant ball of gas—mostly hydrogen, to be exact.

By the 1920s, Eddington had shown that the temperature in the sun's interior had to be in the millions of degrees, which immediately killed any idea that the sun was "on fire." No fire could generate that kind of heat. And then along came Hans Bethe, who solved the mystery.

The awesome power of nuclear fusion drives the sun's heat engine. Here, a huge tongue of fiery gas lashes out from the surface.

The sun and all other stars keep themselves going by a process called nuclear fusion. Every second, the sun converts 700 million tons of hydrogen into helium by forcing protons to combine. Hydrogen atoms contain only one proton and one electron, making hydrogen the simplest element in the universe. (All the others have neutrons.) When temperatures are very high, such as they are inside the sun, the atoms become extremely energetic. In almost no time at all the hydrogen atoms are stripped clean of their electrons, leaving free protons moving around at very fast speeds. This strange gaseous state is called a *plasma*.

If the sun were not so hot and if the protons were not moving so fast, they would never ever dream of trying to stick together. Protons, remember, are electrically charged, and particles that carry the same charge repel each other— a lot like the bumper cars at an amusement park. However, the protons in the sun are traveling at such incredibly high speeds, the strong force takes over the instant the particles collide, causing them to stick together. And then a very curious thing happens. The protons do a quick presto-changeo and turn into three all-new, completely different particles. A magic show on the subatomic level.

In a split second, the crash-victim protons become a deuterium nucleus, a positron, and a neutrino. Deuterium is often called heavy hydrogen. Maybe you can guess why. . . . Okay, time's up. Where a hydrogen nucleus has just one measly proton, a deuterium nucleus has a proton *and* a neutron, and it's the weight of the neutron that makes the hydrogen heavy. Positrons, the second type of particle produced in the collision, are a cheap imitation of the electron. They look almost exactly like electrons, but instead of having a negative charge, positrons are positive (more about positrons in Chapter 6).

The third and certainly the weirdest particle is the neutrino. When neutrinos are standing still (something they almost never do), they have no mass. This puts them in the same category as the invisible man. They exist, all right, but they don't weigh anything. So neutrinos bulk up by moving—*really* moving! Neutrinos know only one speed—as fast as light, and this gives them the ability to pass through pretty much anything they want.

Astronomers have been trying to trap neutrinos, but the hotshot little things are either too fast or too sneaky. Since nuclear fusion supposedly produces neutrinos, scientists expect a fair amount of them to be coming from the sun. So mostly to test the theory, several years ago astronomers built what they figured was a foolproof neutrino-catcher in the town of Lead, South Dakota. It is a gigantic tank of cleaning fluid buried deep underground, buried so deep, in fact, that the neutrinos would have to be slowed and eventually stopped by all that rock. But the slippery neutrinos seem to be putting one over on the astronomers because to date, very, very few of them have been detected floating around in the cleaning fluid.

Could something be wrong with the instruments? Maybe. Maybe the astronomers are a little off in the neutrino part of the theory too, but they are absolutely certain about one thing: Fusion produces energy. While the sun is slowly changing all its hydrogen into helium through fusion, it is also converting 5 million tons of this very same hydrogen into pure energy *every second of every day*. That amounts to a staggering 390,000,000,000,000,000,000,000,000 watts—enough to power four septillion 100-watt light bulbs. Such is the extraordinary muscle of nuclear fusion, and it is clean energy, without nasty by-products such as gamma radiation.

Well, well, well, said the rocket scientists. What have we here? A power source?

One of the most beautiful and romantic spaceship designs to make use of nuclear fusion came out of England in the 1970s. The creators were the engineers of the British Interplanetary Society (BIS), founded forty years earlier in 1933. Their dream ship was called *Daedalus*, after the clever inventor of Greek mythology.

Daedalus was originally conceived as a highly sophisticated robot, a crewless probe that would make a flyby of Barnard's star, just under six light-years away. Barnard's star was a tempting target. Some years before, the American astronomer Edward Barnard had detected a little wobble in the path of the star known as Munich 15040.

Astronomers chart star paths by playing an elaborate connect-the-dots game. They take several photographs of the star over a long period of time, carefully marking the star's position in the sky. Then they connect the dots. The path should be a fairly straight line as the star moves through the heavens.* But when Barnard connected the dots for Munich 15040, he found a wavy line, like a strand of curly hair.

Barnard then did some very delicate and, as it turned out later, controversial calculations, and suggested that perhaps something big was tugging on Munich 15040. He theorized that the object was about as big as Jupiter and was orbiting Munich 15040 the way Jupiter orbits the sun. You can't see it through the telescope, said Barnard. It's too small, too dark, and much too far away, but it's there, all right. That wobble in Munich 15040 is a dead giveaway.

But what exactly was this mysterious object? A planet? The first extrasolar planet ever found? Or nothing more than a

---

*Thanks to good old Newton, again, whose first law says, "An object in motion will tend to remain in motion in a straight line. . . ."

glitch in Barnard's calculations? No one could say, and the matter still hasn't been settled, but wow! What an exciting destination for a spaceship!

Barnard's star is also within range for a spacecraft whose peak velocity would not be more than 100 million miles an hour—15 percent light speed. When we add five years for acceleration, *Daedalus*'s ETA becomes 36 years. That sounds like a very long time, but the distances between the stars are enormous, and in galactic terms, 100 million miles an hour is not so fast. Furthermore, because *Daedalus* would be traveling all by itself, it would have to notify us by radio signal when it arrived. *Daedalus*'s message would rush home at light speed, the fastest it could go, but it would still take nearly 6 years to get here. That makes a grand total of 42 years spent doing absolutely nothing but waiting, pacing the floor, and wondering what *Daedalus* would find when it finally reached its destination.

Who would receive the signal from *Daedalus?* The BIS engineers knew that most of them would not live long enough to hear about *Daedalus*'s adventures in outer space. If the average age of the team was forty years old, the scientists would be in their eighties when the first faint signals began arriving. Nobody wanted to be a pessimist, but nobody was willing to plan that far in advance either. So it was felt that *Daedalus*'s discoveries would probably be left to the next generation.

Truly, this was the best anybody could do. Only one star system is closer to us than Barnard's star, and that is the Centauri triple: Alpha, Beta, and Proxima. But by going to the Centauris, we would shave only about 1.5 light-years off the total distance, and the chances of Alpha, Beta, and Proxima having any planets—as bunched together as they are—

are quite slim. Tidal forces from the mutual gravitation of the three stars would very likely have prevented any planets from forming. So when everything was added up, Barnard's star turned out to be the best candidate, and the engineers got to work.

Daedalus was perhaps one of the very first ships to be designed with a fusion pulse engine. Unlike the fission pulse spacecraft in which the nuclear explosions occur directly behind the vehicle and then rebound off a pusher plate, *Daedalus*'s mini hydrogen bombs would be detonated *inside* a reaction chamber. The hot plasma would then be funneled out to provide thrust. The pulse would come from 250 individual explosions every second, fast enough to be pretty much an unbroken stream. So if *Daedalus* were ever to carry passengers, there wouldn't be any need for shock absorbers.

But one of the biggest problems facing the *Daedalus* team was initiating the atomic reactions. The scientists could not simply put some hydrogen atoms together in a pot and wait for them to fuse. There has to be a trigger of some kind. The hydrogen needs a little encouragement. To date, the only thing we know of that will get hydrogen fusion going is heat, and heat on a very grand scale. A few million degrees would certainly do it.

Now, this is not small potatoes. A few million degrees is almost unthinkably high. The center of the sun where fusion takes place is a few million degrees. How on Earth were the scientists going to come up with that kind of a heat source? They knew that an increase in pressure causes a rise in temperature, but four or five million degrees was more than they could manage with the equipment they had. In fact, there was absolutely nothing that could even get close to generating the required heat. . . . Unless you counted atomic bombs.

Uranium fission produces enormous temperatures, but along with the heat comes dangerous gamma radiation. The BIS scientists had no intention of designing a clean fusion engine only to fire it up with some dirty bombs. For one thing, *Daedalus* would not have been allowed to take off within the Earth's atmosphere because of the Nuclear Test Ban Treaty. For another, *Daedalus* would have had to be fitted with extensive lead shielding to protect its sensitive instruments. So with the nuclear bomb idea nixed, BIS had no choice but to fiddle around with the fusion itself.

Strictly speaking, fusion occurs when the nuclei of two atoms are made to combine, producing a larger, heavier nucleus. Nowhere in the recipe is there anything about which nuclei you have to use. The sun fuses hydrogen because that's all it has. Gradually, this hydrogen is being converted into helium, and after a few billion years, the sun will be made entirely of helium. And then what? Will the sun shut down? Will it click off like a burned-out light bulb? No. Once again, the sun will simply use what it has; this time, the helium. In the second part of its life span, the sun will begin to fuse the helium atoms, and when the helium is all gone, it will start on its newly manufactured beryllium. In fact, the sun will keep right on going, fusing whatever happens to be available until it hits a dead end with carbon.

Well, now, thought the BIS scientists. As long as we're not locked into hydrogen, let's try something a little bit easier to manage. How about combining deuterium and helium-3 flash-frozen into little pellets? The deuterium and helium-3 pellets would be kept in separate tanks and shot, one of each at a time, into a large reaction chamber. There the pellets would be zapped with a high-power electron beam that would force an enormous amount of energy on a very tiny area. The resulting pressure would cause the pellets to implode. An *im*plosion is an *ex*plosion in reverse. Instead of matter and energy bursting outward, it all comes together very quickly at the center. This would raise the temperature of the pellets and force the nuclei to fuse. The reaction chamber would then be filled with an extremely hot and very energetic plasma. The plasma would react with a strong magnetic field that would force it out of the rear of the spacecraft. This would provide the exhaust mass to drive *Daedalus.*

In the original design, the ship had a single stage and needed five years to accelerate to 15 percent light speed. But *Daedalus I* turned out to be much too heavy. Its reaction chamber alone had a diameter larger than three football fields placed end zone to end zone. *Daedalus I* would have used an awful lot of fuel and been too inefficient to be practical.

The final design was much better, but the engineers had to make compromises. Instead of a 40-year journey, *Daedalus* would take its time, arriving at Barnard's star 54 years after launch. Speed would be cut too. *Daedalus*'s peak cruising velocity would be just under 13 percent light speed, not quite 88 million miles an hour. Launch would be from either lunar or Jupiter orbit where escape velocity is much lower than from the Earth's surface.

There really wasn't too much wrong with *Daedalus.* A minor problem was the scarcity of helium-3, but there were ways to get around it. One scientist suggested a fusion reaction involving hydrogen and boron. Although this would mean higher ignition temperatures, it could be achieved through microexplosions. But for all the hard work and careful planning, *Daedalus* never got off the ground. Barnard's star, still 5.9 light-years away, continues to wait for its first envoy from planet Earth.

The Daedalus *starship*

THE BRITISH INTERPLANETARY SOCIETY

And if it is waiting for humans, it will surely not see them emerge from the hatch of a *Daedalus*. *Daedalus* may have looked terrific with its spherical fuel tanks and spidery framework. Snub-nosed and squat, it was very different from all the other ships being designed at the time. While the *Saturn V* and even Orion smacked of Buck Rogers and Flash Gordon, *Daedalus* was exotic, a little alien even, and seemed to hold all the promises of interstellar journeys deep within its massive engine bay. But it was never meant to be.

The BIS engineers had left something out. In none of the hundreds of drawings and plans was any provision ever made for a *Daedalus* crew. There were no bunks, no galley, no recreation area. And there were no portholes through which the daring adventurers from planet Earth could watch the stars as they drifted through space on their long, long journey.

At its very swiftest, *Daedalus* needed fifty-four years to reach its target. Flyby would be almost a blur, faster than a speeding bullet at almost 88 million miles an hour. Barnard's star would loom up suddenly out of the darkness and then be gone, steadily receding, getting smaller and smaller until it was a dot of silver among the thousands of other stars.

On and on *Daedalus* would fly, never slowing down or stopping. For eternity, the little craft would make its way through galaxy after galaxy with the universe expanding in front of it. And in the eye blink that is time on such a monstrous scale, the *Daedalus* crew, if it had had one, would have crumbled to dust.

Fifty-four years to Barnard's star under optimum conditions, with an extremely limited payload and no passengers. Fifty-four years without time to decelerate. Fifty-four years *one way.* With a crew aboard, the journey out would be much, much longer, perhaps one hundred years. A crew needs more than a ship; it needs a safe, comfortable place to live. *Daedalus* would have to be outfitted with air and water purification systems, waste treatment, food supplies and farming areas, heat, light, medical facilities, emergency survival systems. The craft would grow steadily in size and mass and become increasingly harder to accelerate to the desired speed. The engineers would see their 12 percent light speed chipped away to perhaps 10 percent or 9 percent.

Who would go to Barnard's star then? "Good-bye forever," the crew would whisper. Good-bye to everything they ever knew, to their friends and family, to all other human contact except the five or six other intrepid volunteers willing to forsake all of Earth for a moment passing another star. Who would go?

Maybe no one at all.

And to send *Daedalus* still farther into the galaxy without a crew would be almost folly. Consider the stars in our immediate neighborhood. They are the three Centauris at just over four light-years. They are the brilliant white star Sirius A and its tiny companion, Sirius B. They are Wolf 359 and Lalande 21185, a dim reddish star which seems to have something dark in orbit around it. They are Epsilon Eridani and 61 Cygni. And there are a handful of others, known only by numbers and a series of elaborate measurements. They lie scattered through the heavens out to about eleven light-years from Earth—within our grasp, but just barely.

At 13 percent light speed, a *Daedalus* craft, or something similar, would need about eighty years to reach a star eleven light-years away. Add to that five years for acceleration to cruising speed plus eleven years for the return signal, and a single journey to a not-so-very-distant place becomes a century-long trek. The engineers who built the craft, who programmed it and outfitted it and watched it lift off from Earth, would not live long enough to see the fruits of their labors. Five or six years of frenzied activity preparing for the great launch would be followed by many decades of waiting. The sons and daughters of the original scientists, the students of the first *Daedalus* engineers, would also probably never learn what happened when the ship reached its target. The faint signals beamed from so very far away would be left to a third, and maybe even a fourth, generation to decipher. And after such a long, long time, would anybody still be listening?

But perhaps saddest of all is the chance that in a century's time we would have built better and faster spaceships. It is entirely possible that a shiny new craft, traveling at 50 percent, 60 percent, or even 90 percent light speed would outstrip *Daedalus* and reach the target first. Like the tortoise and the hare, the speedy ship from the twenty-second century would race past *Daedalus*, banners flying, trailing a wake of antimatter explosions, or light beams, or something even more exotic.

Thirteen percent light speed sounds fast, but for a craft whose destination is even nine light-years away, 13 percent is slower than a crawl. Vega, a brilliant white star around which a solar system may be forming, is much too far at twenty-six light-years. Even Tau Ceti, a strong candidate for planets, is nearly out of range at just twelve light-years.

The universe is inconceivably large and dotted sparsely with stars. A vast nothingness predominates, and to cross this gulf, this great expanse of everdark, we will need something far more inventive than a *Daedalus*. Even if we could solve all the problems associated with a fusion pulse ship, we would still not be able to take it much beyond our own solar system and live to tell the glorious tales of space travel. So *Daedalus* was eventually laid to rest.

If we could go to the stars on dreams alone, we would surely have been there already. But we must play according to the rules of the game, and the rules, as Newton and Einstein have explained them, are strict and unforgiving. Reaction mass . . . exhaust velocity . . . thrust . . . fuel supply . . . payload . . . acceleration . . . speed of light . . . Building a spaceship is a grand balancing act where dreams create but numbers rule.

And so, said the scientists, maybe we ought to quit trying to go so fast. Maybe it's time we built something slow and lumbering, something that uses its fuel sparingly and isn't in so much of a hurry.

Maybe it's time we built an ark. ★

CHAPTER 4

★

Noah's Ark Meets
the Galaxy

*N*oah had a tough assignment. He had to construct a huge, leakproof vessel according to some pretty demanding specifications. And then (as if that weren't enough), Noah, who was over six hundred years old at the time, was supposed to go out and find samples of every living animal on the Earth, select two of each, and haul them all down to the building site. It must have been a mob scene! But by launch day the passenger list was full and complete, and Noah was ready to roll.

Noah's ark was a masterpiece of engineering—strong, watertight, and completely self-contained—which was a good thing, because the upcoming trip was promising to be a real corker. Noah and the animals would be plowing through driving rain, floods, and freezing darkness. For months nobody would be able to leave the ark or even stick their heads outside. All the familiar sights of home would be gone. The trees and houses and villages, the vineyards and orchards would be forever left behind, part of a world to which the arkians could never again return.

But if Noah was sad or nervous about the adventure, he didn't show it. Into the mighty ark he and the animals climbed. Perhaps Noah took one last look around. "Goodbye," he may have whispered, and then gently bolted the great gopherwood door. And the rest, as they say, is history—the history of space flight.

Things were not going well at the rocket factory. So much emphasis on speed . . . Why, it was enough to drive an engineer nuts. Try to crank up the engines so the crew doesn't die on the way and all of a sudden there are problems with the fuel. You need tons of it! And just where are you supposed to put it? So everybody starts looking around for some super lightweight fuel that won't hog all the available space on the ship, and they wind up drifting into the realm of science fiction.

"All right, hold it!" cried a handful of scientists who certainly knew when enough was enough. "Instead of wasting all our energy trying to design an interstellar racehorse, why don't we make something more along the lines of a galactic turtle?"

Surely they had to be joking.

But no, these maverick scientists insisted, they were absolutely serious. Their plan was to build a space ark, a huge ship like the kind that Noah made, only with a modest engine that can drive it at, say, a couple of percent light speed. Then five hundred, maybe a thousand people all climb aboard and live in the ark until it reaches the target star.

But the other scientists had a few concerns. "How far is this target star?" someone wanted to know.

"A hundred light-years. Maybe a thousand light-years. What does it matter?"

"Won't the passengers die on the way?"

"Well, of course they'll die. They're not robots. That's not the point. You see, the arkians will have babies. The babies will grow up and have more babies, just like on Earth. Don't you get it? The ark is a generation ship. The population keeps on replacing itself. And then, sometime far in the future, the ship at last makes planetfall. Yes, the original arkians have long ago died out, but beings from planet Earth have still made it across the great gulf of space. Presto! We've conquered the distance problem! So what do you think?"

Well, actually, the scientists didn't think it was a bad idea at all. In fact, they've more or less been kicking it around since the Russian rocketman Konstantin Tsiolkovsky first proposed the concept of a space ark in 1928. But unfortunately, the world wasn't ready to do much about space anythings in 1928. Robert Goddard had only just launched his little liquid-fueled rocket a couple of years before (it was shorter than he was), and *Sputnik* was still thirty years in the future. So space exploration was left up to the science fiction magazines.

For fifteen cents you could have bought the November 1939 issue of *Startling Stories* and escaped pre–World War II in the monstrous red, yellow, and blue Ark of Space featured on the cover. Partly the design of the story's author and partly the fantasy of the staff artist, the arks were pretty eye-catching stuff, just what a publisher needed to boost magazine sales. But stripped of their garish crayon colors and ornamental doodads, all the space arks were really just big, multi-leveled ships. Like Noah's prototype, an ark can easily accommodate 1,000, 5,000, even 10,000 passengers. It leaves Earth with a finite amount of air and water, basic necessities that the arkians will probably never be able to replace. So the air must constantly be cleaned of pollutants and carbon dioxide, and recirculated (after all, the passengers can't open the windows), and the water must be treated so it can be used again and again.*

None of this, though, is a problem as long as the population on the ark remains constant to within a few individuals. If births begin to greatly outnumber deaths, the closed, extremely fragile environment of the ark will become threatened. There simply won't be enough water to go around. Living space—that very precious commodity—will shrink. The air may become saturated with carbon dioxide, which will in turn mean that more green plants will have to be grown—not so serious as long as there's room for them. But all these additional people will be eating more food, straining the labs and agricultural areas. So ark planners have recommended that the ship be outfitted to support between 1,000 and 5,000 people. But most likely, the ark will leave Earth with a much smaller core population. This will allow a comfortable "birth leeway."

Early on, life in the ark will seem strange and a little unsettling. Despite the careful screening of applicants and the months of orientation prior to departure, the travelers will still be Earthlings. They will have been thrust into what amounts to a rather large chamber with windows that don't open, artificial sunlight, recycled air, and the cold, hard fact that they will never in all their lives see Earth again. That's a pretty scary proposition. So every effort will be made to create the illusion that the ark is just another small town.

---

*Science has already made great strides turning waste water into perfectly safe drinking water. First the solids are removed by filtration. Then the water is purified with something such as radioactive cobalt. The result is actually cleaner, more bacteria-free than the stuff that is currently coming out of your faucet.

Young couples will marry and, within certain guidelines, have children. If the ark were to leave Earth filled to capacity, the wait for a birth slot could be a decade or more. Think about it: Who would be the most likely passengers? Chances are they will be young and middle-aged people. Grandpa Skuggs may be too old and fragile to go into space. Granny Fitz may not want to leave her little white clapboard house. So if the most senior Earth/arkian is in his or her sixties, a twenty-five-year-old couple might have to wait until they are in their forties before they are allowed to start a family.

Some years ago, Princeton University physicist Gerard O'Neill gave science—and the rest of us—a glimpse of what he believed an orbiting space colony should look like. A space colony is basically an ark that doesn't go anywhere. It is built, part by part, on Earth, and then the parts are hauled into orbit where they are assembled. The finished colonies circle the Earth like artificial moons and, depending on their size, would even be visible through binoculars or a small telescope. O'Neill's colonies range from a very modest half mile in length to something as big as a typical town on Earth, measuring twenty miles from end to end. The colonies are huge cylinders that roll slowly like logs to simulate gravity.

O'Neill's colonies never got past the design stage, but recently Dr. Gregory Matloff suggested stringing a couple of the smaller models together to form a space ark. This would make the Matloff/O'Neill ark more than a mile and a quarter long with the two cylinders joined in the center by fuel tanks and engines. Propulsion would be achieved by a fusion pulse engine fueled by deuterium and helium-3. Top cruising velocity would be just 1 percent light speed.

Math speedos will have already figured out that 1 percent light speed is maybe enough to overtake a turtle on one of his slow days. It is about 6.5 million miles an hour, not bad if you're planning a weekend trip to Mars, but ridiculous for anything farther. If the ark is launched at the turn of the twenty-first century, Matloff calculates that it would not reach Alpha Centauri—a measly 4.3 light-years away—until the middle of the twenty-sixth century! That's somewhere in the vicinity of 2550! During that time the ark would have been home to at least thirteen generations.

But, okay, you might be thinking, isn't a space ark deliberately designed to be a long-term ship? Don't the voyagers sign on knowing they will be star cruising for umpteen years? Certainly, but consider Matloff's destination. It is a triple star system around which not a single planet has ever been detected. In fact, tidal forces created by the three stars may have actually prevented planets from forming. So now along comes an ark that has been plodding through the pitch blackness of space for five hundred years. The voyagers are desperate to set foot on a real, honest-to-goodness planet. But as the ship draws closer and closer to the triple Centauri system, its mighty telescopes reveal nothing, not even a craggy asteroid circling the dim little stars. Even worse, Proxima seems to be emitting X rays.

Can things get any worse? Yes, indeed, they certainly can. Consider the following scenarios.

Despite its slow crawl through space, the ark has used up all its fuel. It is now trapped in orbit around one of the Centauri stars. Terrified by their grim fate, the arkians immediately send a distress call. Then they prepare to wait. The message takes 4.3 years to reach Earth. Another 4.3 years pass before an answer is received by the arkians.

REGRET YOUR SITUATION STOP NO BACKERS FOR LONG-DISTANCE SPACE FLIGHT STOP HANG TOUGH STOP TRY US AGAIN IN TWENTY YEARS STOP

Or . . .

The cold winds of despair fill the ark, and a killing apathy settles down around the passengers-turned-permanent-residents. We have been on a fool's errand, they think. There are no planets, and now we are left to circle endlessly. With little left to care about, the passengers gradually begin to ignore some of the ark's restrictions.

One young woman becomes pregnant without permission. Then another. Then a third. Before long, the population aboard the ark swells to frightening proportions. Soon, overcrowding threatens everyone's existence. Violence breaks out, and for the first time in half a millennium, murders occur. Arkian society disintegrates. The water supply is fouled, the air is polluted, and the downward spiral cannot be stopped. Long before the turn of the century, the arkians perish, every last one. And because space is a near vacuum, a derelict ship from planet Earth remains in silent orbit around Beta Centauri forever.

Or . . .

Within a century after the original ark is launched, a major technological breakthrough occurs that allows us to achieve 99.999 percent light speed. Within fifty years, a ship is built and sent to Alpha Centauri. It passes the ark both going out and returning home!

So now what are we to make of this space ark business? Doesn't sound so good, does it? But many of the ark's original admirers refused to throw in the towel. They had another idea. . . .

In the 1960s Stanley Kubrick and science fiction writer Arthur C. Clarke gave us quite an eyeful on the big screen. In their classic film *2001: A Space Odyssey*, they showed us a silent, almost eerie solution to the distance problem. As the camera came in for a tight shot, it revealed a small group of sleeping astronauts, temporarily entombed in gleaming white coffinlike pods. Soft ice crystals lined the sleepers' brows and lashes, and the faces looked cooly serene. Monitors above the pods displayed each sleeper's heartbeat and respiration, and an elaborate medi-computer kept the sleepers' strange environment consistent with life.

You didn't have to be a rocket scientist to know what Kubrick and Clarke were proposing here. The astronauts aboard *Discovery I* bound for one of Jupiter's moons were cryonically frozen. Prior to launch or very early in the voyage, they were placed in the pods and their body temperatures lowered to just around the freezing point. There they would remain, suspended between life and death, dreamlessly asleep, never aging, waiting out the days and hours and months. At journey's end, HAL, the ship's computer, would revive the sleepers by gradually restoring warmth to their bodies.

It is now twenty years later, and the setting is not a Hollywood soundstage with molded plastic and Styrofoam, but California—the real one. An Oakland company called Trans Time is offering a daring doorway to death, and ice is the key. For the onetime fee of a hundred thousand dollars, Trans Time will freeze you solid at the moment of cardiac death. Then, ever so carefully—and it must be carefully or your icy-stiff body will shatter—the Trans Time technicians will wrap you in aluminum foil and slip you into a huge plastic bag. After a quick dunking in a vat of dry ice, you will be strapped to a pallet and slid into what is essentially a gigantic thermos bottle. This "forever flask," as it is called, will then be filled to the brim with liquid nitrogen cooled to a rather stimulating minus 320 degrees Fahrenheit. The cap will be secured and the flask hung upside down. This is not some kind of tasteless joke but a safety measure. Should the nitrogen level in your bottle suddenly begin to drop, your head would be the last to thaw out.

Sounds like science fiction, but for a hundred thousand dollars (as of this writing), it is certainly real enough. Trans Time promises to top off your thermos bottle periodically to

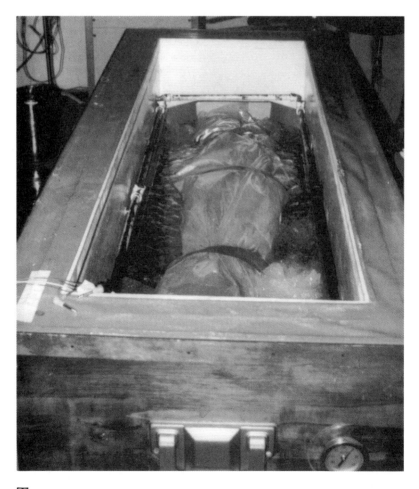

*T*he dry-ice dunk at Trans Time. Someday, frozen may be the way to go very great distances.

keep you freezer fresh, and they will do this for as long as it takes science to figure out how to bring you back to life. Science also has the added burden of coming up with a cure for whatever killed you. No small potatoes.

Now, the eerie goings-on at the Trans Time facilities may send shivers up your spine, but what these people are attempting to do is very much within the spirit of space travel and the *2001* sleep pods. They are trying to freeze an entire body without damaging any of the organs. The hoped-for result would be a perfectly preserved human being who could—if science ever gets that far—actually be revived.

Naturally, we are not planning to send dead bodies into space with the hopes that some advanced alien civilization will board the ship and bring everybody back to life. The idea instead is to find a foolproof way to put living space travelers into a deep cryonic state, à la Kubrick and Clarke in *2001: A Space Odyssey.* This would be the ultimate in suspended animation. Whole body freezing would literally put the lives of the passengers on hold. The "ice sleepers" would not take a breath or experience a single heartbeat. They would have no pulse. Brain neurons would stop firing. Kidneys would not produce urine or stomachs digestive acids. Absolutely every cell in the sleepers' bodies would cease to function in a kind of death-but-not-death.

As their starship sailed the light-years, the passengers would lie in their ice cocoons, defying time. The ark could travel at 1 percent light speed, inching its way toward Alpha Centauri or even the Andromeda galaxy over 2 million light-years away.* Miles and the endless stretch of the universe

---

*Obviously, at a measly 1 percent light speed, a trip to the Andromeda galaxy is going to take quite a long time, and some as yet unspecified provisions would have to be made for maintaining the ship. Things will break and wear out and ultimately need replacement.

---

would become meaningless. Freezing would make us the ultimate star traveler.

There is also a very practical side to all this. For almost the whole voyage, only a small skeleton crew of maintenance workers would be eating the food and drinking the water aboard the ark. Vast areas would not have to be given over to farming and agriculture. Much less water would be needed. (Water adds substantial weight to the ship.) With upwards of 95 percent of the passengers occupying a space only slightly bigger than themselves, the ark layout could be more efficient, more compact. The builders might even decide to eliminate the artificial gravity in all but a few key places.

If you're starting to think that frozen solid is definitely the way to travel to distant star systems, you're not alone. A number of scientists have seriously been kicking around the idea of suspended animation. But as it so often happens, scientific enthusiasm is far outstripping scientific achievement.

To date, doctors and researchers have had extremely limited success with freezing techniques. They have managed only the simplest, least complicated body parts like blood, tissues, corneas, ova and sperm, and embryos in tiny clusters of four to eight cells. This is hardly enough to send into space.* The Red Cross in particular would love to be able to freeze entire organs and store them for future transplant patients. But the best the Red Cross can do is to pack the

---

*A number of years ago, science fiction author Ben Bova suggested sending frozen embryos into space with a small crew of adults. As the ship neared the target star, the embryos would be defrosted and brought to term in artificial wombs. Wait a few years, and *bam!* instant crew, just in time to take over for the aging adults. But medical science has not caught up to Bova, and currently we haven't the slightest idea how to build an artificial womb. But maybe more important, would we even want to?

hearts, lungs, kidneys, and livers in dry ice, rush them to the operating room, and hope they make it before tissue death renders the organ unusable.

Maybe because we're so used to popping those extra slices of pizza into the freezer, we wonder why we can't pop ourselves into the freezer too. But pizza is dough, tomato sauce, cheese, and maybe a few anchovies, and we, unquestionably, are not. A frozen person can't be revived with ten minutes in a 450-degree preheated oven.

One of the problems is our very high water content. We are, in fact, about 70 percent water—the liquid of life at room temperature, but the kiss of death if it is allowed to freeze.

Water, as you know, turns to ice when the temperature falls to 32 degrees Fahrenheit. This in itself is not so bad, but ice is a crystal. Its molecules have a regular repeating geometric shape with straight sides and sharp angles. Look closely at a snowflake. A snowflake is a single crystal of ice. Its pattern may be beautiful, but its pointy edges would be deadly to fragile cell walls. If you think of a cell as a water balloon, the ice crystal is the pin. As the forming ice begins its advance it tears at cells and tissues, "poking holes" and eventually destroying the body beyond repair. And if that's not enough to do you in, there's always the expansion factor.

You may have learned the hard way that ice takes up more room than the same amount of water. This is because water expands as it freezes. Ice power will not only blow the top off a sealed soda bottle, but it can also explode the bottle. Concrete roads crack and split like freshly baked muffins when water that has seeped into the ground freezes during the winter. So just imagine what would happen to a human cell—which is mostly water—when the body's temperature is lowered to 32 degrees Fahrenheit. The cell, just like the soda bottle, would explode. Now, multiply that times several billion cells and you can easily see the problem with trying to freeze a whole person.

But hold on here. It is a well-known fact among zoologists and animal behaviorists that frogs can withstand some pretty icy conditions. In fact, they have been found buried in the mud with as much as 50 percent of their body frozen solid. Heartbeat, respiration, digestion—the works!—were effectively shut down until conditions improved. Then the frogs just thawed out naturally. And even more impressive is the ordinary, run-of-the-mill, common housefly who easily gets through temperatures that plunge into the teens. But before you say, "Oh, well, come on. Flies are just bugs," take a gander at what surely must be considered birdland's Mr. Cool. It is the Arctic willow gull, able to withstand up to sixty degrees below zero! That's good enough to survive on Mars. (Provided, of course, that the gull brings along his own oxygen.)

Okay. It's a trick, right? Yes, but it took scientists quite some time to discover just what the trick was. These animals, along with a surprising number of others, have a secret ingredient in their bloodstream. It is called glycerol,* a syrupy sweet alcohol that prevents water from forming crystals when it freezes. Instead, the water turns into a glassy solid, smooth-edged and very gentle on delicate cell walls. Everything freezes, but nothing breaks.

Glycerol would certainly seem to be the answer to our space ark prayers if it weren't for one rather disturbing side effect. Glycerol and its laboratory relative propylene glycol are extremely toxic to humans.

The Red Cross has tried infusing kidneys with propylene

---

*It's pronunciation time again. **GLIS** ER UL

64

glycol, and they say, so far, so good, but they do not yet know if the organs will function safely and efficiently once they are transplanted. So for now at least, frozen astronauts will have to remain just a bit of Hollywood trickery.

But if we can't turn our space voyagers into ice cadets, maybe we can get away with chilling them down a little. Instead of 32 degrees, what about 42 degrees? What about good old-fashioned, my-brother-the-ground-squirrel-does-it-all-the-time hibernation?

Ever since the Earth has known cold weather, there have been some animals that were too lazy to migrate to warmer climes. These are the hibernators, the bats and ground squirrels who can lower their body temperature, practically stop their breathing and heartbeat, put the skids on their metabolism, and sack out for the winter. For six, seven, even eight months out of the year, the hibernators remain all but motionless, rousing themselves only occasionally and for brief periods of time to either take a few cleansing breaths or nibble a little on their stash of food.

Hibernators are not in suspended animation. Their body systems are still functioning, but things are moving along v-e-r-y slowly. Outside, the days and weeks are going by at the old, familiar rate. In the spring, perhaps, the animal will celebrate his second birthday, but after all that hibernating, his body will be much younger than two years old. Through the wondrous process of hibernation, the animal will have, in a sense, outfoxed time. Maybe it's not as good as a nice, long cryogenic sleep, but a crew of hibernating astronauts could certainly put some serious distance behind them.

However, hibernation is a gift that nature has, for some mysterious reason, given to very few animals, and we are not the lucky ones. So in an effort to learn the difference between the haves and have-nots, biologists entered the world of hibernation with their hypodermic needles and microscopes. Operating on the theory that perhaps some chemical in the animal triggers a hibernation response, the scientists withdrew blood from hibernating woodchucks. They then injected a monkey named Spock (appropriately enough) with the woodchuck blood, and to their absolute astonishment Spock slowly but surely went into a kind of prehibernation ritual. He lost interest in food, began to yawn, and literally could not keep his eyes open. Within a few hours, Spock was slumped in his chair peacefully snoozing.

But there's more. When the experimenters took Spock's temperature, they found it had dropped several degrees. Spock's heart rate had fallen from a normal 150 beats per minute to just 75. Was Spock hibernating? The scientists will not commit themselves, but Spock's unusual behavior certainly suggests that a shot of woodchuck blood might be just the stuff to induce hibernation.

A daring question now arises: Would it work on us?

To date, scientists have no plans to test the "hibernation induction trigger," or HIT, as it is called, on humans, mainly because they aren't really sure what it is. Research has suggested HIT might be some kind of protein molecule that stimulates the part of the brain governing the manufacture of natural opiates. Opiates are chemicals that calm us down and make us sluggish and sleepy. This in turn may start a whole chain of events to slow breathing and heartbeat, halt digestion, and shut down metabolism. Finally, when all the trigger chemicals have delivered their messages, hibernation results.

It is awfully exciting to imagine a time when a space ark filled with hibernating galactic voyagers leaves Earth for a star hundreds of light-years away. Through the long, dark journey, robodocs will monitor the hibernators' vital functions and periodically inject them with HIT. Then, a few months short of planetfall, the HIT will be stopped and the travelers allowed to awaken naturally. While it is true that hibernation is not as good as cryonic freezing for holding up the aging process, the star travelers will definitely be younger than their friends and relatives at home who didn't hibernate. With hibernation extending lives as much as 50 percent or more, a one-hundred-year journey becomes quite possible indeed.

But are we really ready for this? A space ark—with or without hibernators—leaves Earth for good. Those hardy adventurers who sign on will face some rather bleak prospects: a blind destination, several decades conked out in a strange, dreamless sleep, and no hope whatsoever of seeing Earth again.

It is November 2090 and the *Noah II* is on its maiden—and only—voyage. It is bound for Barnard's star, six light-years away. What do we know about Barnard's star? Practically nothing. Maybe it has planets, maybe it hasn't. Even the mighty Hubble space telescope launched at the end of the twentieth century couldn't pick up that kind of detail.

Will there be any place to land once the *Noah II* arrives? Who knows? And maybe the arkians won't even want to land. Barnard's star is a red dwarf, about one-tenth the sun's mass. It radiates in cool red light, putting out meager amounts of energy. So only a very close planet would have any chance at all of grabbing enough warmth to support life. But would such a planet have been able to hold onto an atmosphere? What about things like stellar flares, flaming arcs of hot gas that burst upward from a star's surface? Or the streams of atomic particles, the so-called "stellar wind," flowing from Barnard's star like the fallout from a monstrous hydrogen bomb? Either of these conditions could make life on a nearby planet less than friendly.

An ark that carries hibernating passengers is an ark that will not travel too far from Earth, or what's the point of plunging everyone into hibernation? Hibernation would be used to extend the lives of the original passengers so that they—not their children or grandchildren—could reach their destination. So by limiting our travel time, we also limit our distance. Of the known stars, only thirteen lie within ten light-years of Earth. This does not give us much choice.

As far as a multigenerational ark is concerned, we're already on one. It is, of course, planet Earth, which cruises around the galaxy, slowly but surely sightseeing other stars. Why, then, would five or six thousand people sign up for basically the same flight in a ship that isn't anywhere near as good?

A number of years after Gregory Matloff suggested turning a couple of O'Neill's space colonies into an ark, he had second thoughts. Matloff saw that his ark—or anyone else's for that matter—would be much too slow to be practical. So Matloff proposed ram charging the ark. Crank it up a little, he said. Get it moving. But that, of course, made the ark just another not-so-very-exciting spaceship, and after a while the idea of an interstellar ark began to slip into the sunset. But as night fell on the slowest idea the rocket scientists ever had, the day was dawning on one of the fastest. . . . ★

CHAPTER 5

★

Bussard's Beauty—
The Interstellar Ramjet

*T*his is the tale of a fabulous ship. It was designed in 1960 by American physicist Dr. Robert Bussard. It is best known as the Bussard ramjet and sometimes the ramscoop, but to all the dreamers of star dreams, it is Bussard's beauty.

Bussard was at the Los Alamos Scientific Laboratory in New Mexico when he came up with what is certainly one of the most out-of-this-world starship designs ever conceived. The principle of the Bussard ramjet is simple and elegant. Instead of dragging along tons and tons of fuel, the ramjet just scoops it up along the way. This eliminates the need for bulky fuel tanks shaped like colossal blimps and allows the ship to be light and sleek and—more importantly—*fast!*

A series of coils generates tremendous magnetic fields that

gather in hydrogen atoms as the ship plows through inter-stellar space. The hydrogen is then channeled into a huge reaction chamber where it is fused into helium. In fusion, as you have seen, massive amounts of energy are produced, and it is this energy that drives the ship. Bussard envisioned the ramjet steadily accelerating until it reached a speed just short of light.

Good-bye lumbering space arks that take forever to go a measly four light-years. With the ramjet shooting along at almost 186,000 miles a second, the magical effects of relativity kick in, and a journey to the center of the galaxy takes just twenty years.

Wow! Pack up the kids and let's go!

Bussard's beautiful idea was received with great enthusi-asm by the rocket community. Science writer Walter Sullivan mentioned the ramjet in his book, *We Are Not Alone,* about communication with alien civilizations. Isaac Asimov and Stephen Dole referred to it in their book, *Planets for Man.* And the artists had a field day with the ramjet's starkly fu-turistic design.

Here was a ship that even Hollywood could love. Sleek and lean, like a long-distance runner, the Bussard ramjet stretches nearly a mile and a half in length. In contrast to the gentle curves of *Daedalus,* the ramjet is arrow straight, and easily dwarfs every other interstellar rocket ever con-ceived. It is nearly twenty times longer than the *Saturn V* and almost as tall as Mount Olympus. So because of its size and Earth weight of over 160,000 tons, the ramjet would certainly have to be assembled in space, piece by piece.

The ramjet's fusion engine is located in the extreme aft of the ship behind a spidery support structure reminiscent of some mighty skyscraper under construction. Wrapped

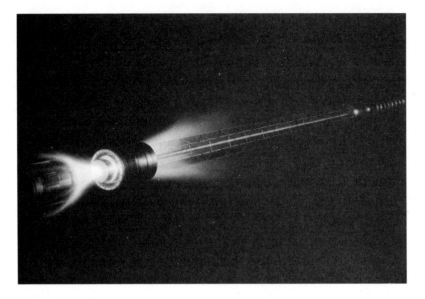

The Bussard ramjet, as sleek as a long-distance runner. The magnetic coils are in the extreme foresection of the ship.

around the engine section are the ramjet's magnetic coils, capable of generating magnetic fields that extend thousands of miles into space. As the ramjet cruises through the darkness, interstellar hydrogen will be trapped by the fields and spiral inward. Then the ship's fusion reactor will turn it all into usable energy. The concept and the physics could not be more elegant, and nearly everybody in the rocket community knew it.

But then, slowly, the mists of all that early enthusiasm began to clear, and a hard reality moved in like an advancing front. Bussard's design was certainly sound. The ship would go, all right, but would we ever actually be able to build it?

Bussard's objective was to have the ramjet steadily accelerate at what is called "one gravity," or 1g for short; 1g is the speed at which Earth's gravity pulls objects downward.

Let's say, for instance, that Bugsy "the Thumb" Baker (captain of the Hot Strikers) rears back and fires his bowling ball at a seven-ten split. But let's also say that Bugsy's release is just a little high, and the ball hits the lane with a ferocious wallop. Gravity, of course, makes Bugsy's ball come crashing down, but at a very definite rate of speed.

During the first second Bugsy's ball is plummeting; it falls thirty-two feet.* So far, so good, but during the second second, a very curious thing happens; Bugsy's ball accelerates. Instead of covering just thirty-two feet, the ball is able to go sixty-four feet. It falls twice as fast as it did during the first second of flight. At the end of second number three, Bugsy's ball has increased its speed by another thirty-two feet, so now its velocity is ninety-six feet a second. And with each additional second that Bugsy's bowling ball is airborne, Earth gravity adds another thirty-two feet to the last distance covered.

Now, fortunately, the bowling alley roof is not high enough and Bugsy is not strong enough to allow a bowling ball to be hurled ninety-six feet into the air (almost ten stories!). So Bugsy's ball is not traveling all that fast when it hits the lane. (For this, the management is very grateful.) And it's also fortunate that, should Bugsy accidentally drop his bowling ball from the tenth-floor window of his apartment building, air resistance will slow the ball's plunge to the ground (although it would still be wise to steer clear of it). But in space things are different. When a rocket accelerates at 1g, it truly does increase its speed by thirty-two feet every second, so it can put some significant distance behind it.

---

*If Bugsy went bowling on the moon, he would find that his bowling ball doesn't fall as fast. That's because moon gravity is much weaker than Earth gravity.

The speed at 1g is ideal for spaceships for two reasons. First, because a 1g acceleration mimics the gravitational pull of the Earth, all the passengers will feel right at home. They won't be bouncing weightlessly around the ship like helium-filled balloons. Second (and certainly more exciting), a ship with an acceleration rate of 1g will come very close to light speed in about one year.

But there's a catch. If we want to keep on increasing our speed, we will have to use more and more fuel. This is one of relativity's weirdo side effects. You would think that going from 0 percent to 45 percent light speed consumes the same amount of fuel as going from 45 percent to 90 percent, but because of the relativity theory, it's not that way at all.

When Einstein was working out his famous equations, he noticed that as objects moved faster and faster through space, they grew more massive—not bigger, mind you, but heavier. It is an absolute fact that when you are riding The Whip at Cosmoland, you weigh just a little bit more than when you are standing in line to buy cotton candy. Of course, nobody around notices your sudden weight gain on The Whip because you're not moving fast enough. But if you were inside a rocket traveling at, say, 99 percent light speed, there'd be quite a difference between your out-of-rocket "rest" weight and your "moving" weight. But even wilder, at exactly light speed, you and your rocket ship would be infinitely heavy!

Question: How do you accelerate an infinitely heavy rocket?

Answer: You use an infinite amount of fuel.

Translation: That's why nothing can be accelerated past the speed of light. There's no such thing as an infinite amount of fuel!

But if we had enough fuel, we should certainly be able to accelerate our ship close to light speed, maybe 186,282 miles a second. (Light speed is 186,282.3976 miles per second.) So this brings us back to Bussard's ramjet, the spaceship with the bottomless fuel tank. The ramjet runs on hydrogen, and hydrogen is by far the most abundant element in the universe. It is found scattered throughout space in wisps and veils, heaped into piles in dense clouds, and is the major component of most stars. Clearly, the hydrogen is there for the scooping—if we have a big enough scoop.

The scoop, or intake, is actually several magnetic coils called solenoids (SOLE IN OYDS). The solenoids generate the powerful magnetic fields that trap the hydrogen atoms as the ship flies on through space. But the ship won't even get out of its own garage unless it is able to collect sufficient quantities of hydrogen on a steady basis. Your car—or at least the hot little number you've been ogling in the showroom window—also needs a continuous supply of fuel in order to run. That's why cars have accelerators; the accelerator provides the engine with fuel.

The ramjet, of course, doesn't burn its fuel. It is driven by fusion reactions, the same fusion reactions that occur inside the sun. During the process, four hydrogen atoms are forced to combine to produce one helium atom, but to do any good, this has to happen countless times, so the supply of hydrogen is critical. The sun, of course, has hydrogen to, er . . . burn, but the ramjet has to go out and look for it. This puts a little pressure on the ramjet's pilot.

In the olden days when trains were called locomotives, they ran on coal. A stoker fed heaping shovelfuls of the stuff into a huge furnace where it was burned to provide the steam to drive the train. The stoker (probably underpaid) had to work almost continuously. No fifteen-minute coffee breaks

The Cone Nebula *in the constellation Monoceros is right out there for the scooping.*
HALE OBSERVATORIES

for him, because while he was sipping his demitasse, the train's fuel supply would be cut off, and in pretty short order, the train would slide to a stop.

"Keep shoveling!" we hear the engineer yell from the window of his cab.

But we would also hear the ramjet's captain order the pilot to "Keep scooping!" The scoop must continuously collect hydrogen, or nuclear fusion will crank rudely to a halt.

If you took a spatula and instead of spreading the icing over a cake, you spread out all the hydrogen in space evenly, you would wind up with about two atoms per cubic centimeter. (That's two atoms inside a square box with sides a quarter-inch high.) Since two atoms per cubic centimeter make a pretty thin hydrogen soup, as ramjet pilot, you wouldn't want to miss a drop. So before you left home, you'd advise the engineers to give the ship a pretty big scoop.

Dr. Bussard has calculated that a ramjet weighing a modest 2,200,000 pounds would need a series of magnetic coils (the scoop) with a radius of about 37 miles! To appreciate how tremendous this is, let's say your arm is the ramjet. The engine for your arm-ramjet is located at your wrist. A bangle bracelet will represent the magnetic coils of the collector. If we let one inch equal one mile, and your wrist has a diameter of two inches, then the bangle bracelet will have a diameter of over six feet! That's bigger than a Hula Hoop! And when translated back into ramjet talk, we have a ship with a collector that's downright monstrous!

Oh, but so what? you may be thinking. We're going to assemble the ramjet in space, right? Things are weightless in space. We can make the coils as big as we want.

Well, actually, no we can't because the bigger we make the magnetic coils, the flimsier they become. The coils are hollow rings. Scientists call them tori. A torus (singular of tori) has the same shape as the rubber tube your little brother wears around his waist when he goes swimming. When you measure the diameter of the tube—or the torus—you will find that part of what you are measuring is the hole in the center. So as the diameter of the torus gets bigger, the hole does too, and, structurally, the torus grows weaker and weaker. There comes a point, of course, when the magnetic coils become just too big and too weak to handle any real stress. The ship accelerates, the stresses build, and the coils break apart.

But Bussard already knows this, so he has suggested setting the coils in motion, rotating them to give them some stability. This will work, but only if we don't plan on accelerating the ship too fast. Anything much beyond ½g is almost certain to do in the coils.

Okay, then, what if we make tougher coils?

That is an excellent idea and should indeed solve the problem, but unfortunately, we don't know of a single material that is lightweight, easily portable, and supertough all rolled into one.

We usually think of steel as incredibly strong. Something tough is "as strong as steel," and Superman is the Man of Steel, but steel isn't our best stuff. Consider, for instance, a little something we can whip up called graphite epoxy. Graphite epoxy is a composite; that is, it is made of more than one kind of material. Graphite epoxy weighs about one-fifth of what steel weighs (for equal volumes), and it is measurably stronger. No, it is not strong enough for a ramjet scoop, but as scientists get better at making composites, they might very well hit upon something that is. So for the time being, we either have to stay home or be content to go much, much slower.

But wait just a minute. Some years ago the suggestion was made by a professor at Louisiana State University to "help out" the hydrogen fusion by using what is called nuclear catalysis. A catalyst is chemistry's Mr. Excitement. It makes things happen by speeding up reactions. So, with a catalyst, nuclear fusion would occur more quickly and efficiently, and the engine and the coils could be a lot smaller—say only about one hundred feet across. But in order to get enough hydrogen atoms, the coils would have to generate some whopping magnetic fields. "This," says Bussard, "would not be impossible—only hard."

Most scientists would agree, however, that the very biggest problem facing the ramjet is the fusion drive. Hydrogen fusion, as you have seen, needs enormous, almost impossible start-up temperatures. This is because the protons we are trying to fuse are positively charged, and like charges won't go near each other. But when we turn up the heat, the atoms begin to move around, and the greater the heat, the faster they move. At a couple or three million degrees, the atoms are moving so fast, instead of bouncing away when they hit, they stick together and we get a fusion. This is what goes on in the sun.

The sun makes it all look so easy, but that's only because the conditions up there are perfect; it's intensely hot! On Earth, or in the reactor room of a spaceship, it's another story. Try as they most certainly have, scientists have yet to figure out how to generate the temperatures necessary for fusion. So some scientists have suggested using deuterium instead of hydrogen.

You already met deuterium—also called heavy hydrogen—in an earlier chapter. Deuterium is not quite as fussy as hydrogen, and it is willing to fuse in cooler temperatures. It also happens that deuterium can be found floating freely in interstellar space, although it is nowhere near as common as hydrogen. Astronomers have estimated that for every

6,700 hydrogen atoms, there is only one deuterium atom—hardly what you might call the mother lode. While it's possible that very dense hydrogen clouds could supply enough deuterium to run the fusion reactors, the ramjet is certain to be in trouble way out there in space where the deuterium density is almost zilch. So hydrogen remains the fuel of choice, despite the fact that we can't quite get anything going with it yet.

There is another option, although it's not nearly as satisfying as the true ramjet. Instead of using a straight hydrogen fusion drive, engineers could focus on a less demanding ram-augmented interstellar rocket—RAIR for short. In the RAIR design, hydrogen gas is swept up by the scoop and then the particles are accelerated to superfast speeds. Particle acceleration is nothing new and has been done for years on Earth inside huge circular speedways called cyclotrons. Naturally, there wouldn't be room for a full-size cyclotron in a spaceship, so the RAIR would have to accelerate the particles by spiraling them in a magnetic field. The field would be generated by means of a nuclear reactor. Once we got the particles going, we could shoot them out of the rear of the spacecraft to provide some pretty impressive thrust. Granted, RAIR would not be able to make the speeds of a pure ramjet, but it could still carry a crew to and from fairly distant stars.

Dr. Bussard, however, is a dreamer, as all true scientists are, and he believes that physics and technology will come through with the missing puzzle pieces and then we can be off. In fact, quite a few highly respected scientists agree with him and have estimated that if all goes well, we should be able to launch a real-life, genuine ramjet in as few as seventy to one hundred years. Wow!

But Bussard cautions future ramjet passengers not to ex-

pect a grand tour of the entire galaxy. In his fabulous scenario, flights will be offered only out to about one thousand
light-years. This is a gigantic volume of space, filled with
perhaps 10 million potential star systems! "Enough," says
Bussard, "to keep us busy for a while."

It has been said that scientists are too conservative. They
wear pocket protectors and slick their hair down with smelly
tonics from the 1950s. They eat calculus equations for breakfast and talk in Greek letters. These guys with the egg-shaped
heads have no imagination. Not one bit.

Dr. Bussard's eyes twinkle. His interstellar duffle bag is
already packed. ★

CHAPTER 6

★

The Exotic Fuel Tank

*I*t was a dark and stormy night. (Well, no, perhaps not. It might very well have been 1:00 or 2:00 in the afternoon.) The eminent physicist Paul Dirac was sitting at his desk working on equations that he hoped would clarify a point of relativity, when all of a sudden he found himself staring at a recipe for a superfast rocket fuel.

Dirac's math had revealed an oddball kind of elementary particle. It looked just like the electron except for one rather strange characteristic. Where the electron has a negative electromagnetic charge, Dirac's particle was showing a positive charge.

A positive charge? you might be thinking. Obviously the thing was a proton!

Well, that was Dirac's initial reaction, but a proton is over a thousand times heavier than an electron; Dirac's particle weighed exactly the same as an electron.

Dirac was stumped. Could this "positive electron" be some new kind of particle? Well, this was certainly something! Here it was only 1928 and science hadn't even discovered the neutron yet. What was next? Negative protons?

Actually, yes, said Dirac two years later when he had formulated his theory. There are probably negative protons too. They're all a part of what Dirac had started to call antimatter. For whatever reason, the universe had apparently created a twin for each of its elementary particles. This would seem to be a big waste of effort, making two versions of the same thing, but the antiparticles are not *quite* identical to the particles. They have, as Dirac discovered through his mathematics, opposite charges. They also have opposite spin.

Paul Dirac found a positive electron and formulated a theory of antimatter.

Like miniature stars and planets, some elementary particles turn furiously on their axes. If a particle turns in a clockwise direction, its antiparticle turns counterclockwise.*

Dirac's antimatter theory was bold and daring. It was, remember, 1930. The movies had only recently started to talk, and the Empire State Building was still on the drawing board. And then, too, there was that little problem of proof. Dirac had not actually seen a positive electron in the flesh. So the scientific community smiled politely at the suggestion of antimatter and went on to other things.

But in 1932, the American physicist Carl Anderson spotted a positive electron (later renamed the positron) in a device called a cloud chamber. Dirac had been right. Antimatter definitely existed. It was just a little scarce, that's all.

But who really cares about antimatter anyway? Isn't it just one of those goofy things that only physicists think are cool? It doesn't actually *do* anything, does it?

It must be admitted in the interests of fair play that no, antimatter doesn't do anything. But then, again, ordinary matter doesn't do anything either. However, if the two should happen to come in contact with each other, you'd better duck because the word *explosion* doesn't even begin to describe it.

What matter and antimatter manage to pull off is a total conversion of mass into energy, courtesy of Einstein's famous recipe $E = mc^2$. This is not to be taken lightly. It is major league physics. Matter is essentially energy but in another form, the way ice is just another form of water. To turn ice into water, all we have to do is add a little heat. But to convert mass directly into energy with nothing left over requires some real muscle.

---

*The particle twins differ in a few other ways, but they are strange and subtle and don't really have any effect on what we see.

Rocket engineers find this rather inconvenient, but as far as the universe is concerned, the plan is a good one. It would hardly do for the Earth, let's say, to be able to pop back and forth between its matter and energy state anytime it felt like it. The Earth is a pretty massive place, and if all the matter were to suddenly change over, the force of the explosion would be felt light-years away. As a feeble comparison, 4½ pounds of matter converted directly to energy would have the equivalent explosive force of 43 million tons of TNT or *several thousand* atomic bombs. A little bit of matter packs quite a wallop.

With Dirac's antimatter made real by the sighting of a positron, there was suddenly a way to pull off the mass/energy conversion trick. Put a hunk of matter in with a hunk of antimatter and let nature take its explosive course. Then it's off to Alpha Centauri, to the Great Nebula in Orion, *to the other side of the galaxy!* because this is the perfect fuel. A little goes a very long way, and is it ever efficient! No waste. No sludge or slag or soot or ash. No leftovers. Just pure energy streaming out of the tail of the ship at speeds breathtakingly close to that of light.

Predictably, the science fiction writers loved Dirac's antimatter, although they weren't really too clear on what it was at first. Many of them thought antimatter was a sort of negative matter. A matter apple falls down; an antimatter apple rises up, pushed away instead of attracted by gravity. Well, the benefits of this were obvious: An antimatter ship could just go right ahead and launch itself.* But most science fiction writers are very conscientious and do their homework, and before long they had gotten it all straightened out. However,

---

*But that's where the fun ended, since the crew would all be made of matter. *Ka-boom!*

---

it wasn't until antimatter had been used to drive the engines of the *Enterprise* on "Star Trek" that it really hit the big time (although Captain Kirk's famous request for "warp speed" was pushing it a little).

But meanwhile, back in the labs—the real ones—antimatter was having a bit of a tough go. Dirac's second particle, the antiproton, was not detected until 1955, and the antineutron was still at large. By now nearly everyone in the physics community embraced the antimatter theory, but few rocket engineers wanted any part of it. Antimatter, they pointed out, was not exactly growing on trees. If it took more than twenty years to find just two measly particles, what were the chances of gathering enough antimatter to run a decent-size starship? "And furthermore," said the rocket designers, "as near as we can tell, the only antimatter anybody's ever seen has been in cloud chambers and particle accelerators. Why haven't we found any positrons in space? Where are they?"

Well, the truth is, antimatter, the wondrous rocket fuel, was nowhere around. Had it been abundant, reasoned the scientists, we would be seeing explosions here, there, and everywhere throughout the cosmos as matter and antimatter bumped into each other. So either antimatter is some artificial thing cooked up in a physics lab or the stuff just vanished.

To which the astronomers replied, "The stuff just vanished."

Once upon a very long time ago (they began) when the universe was .0000000000000000000000000000000001 of a second old, space was filled with weird elementary particles and their corresponding antiparticles. This early universe was astonishingly small and hot beyond our wildest imaginations, but it was not to remain that way for long. Immediately, the young, dot-size universe started to expand and cool down, and as it did, the particles and antiparticles got busy annihilating each other. This happened in less than two seconds.

When the smoke cleared, so to speak, all the antimatter was gone. The universe continued to cool and grow ever larger, and, because initially there had been a bit more matter than antimatter, the universe was able to evolve into what we see today.

This remarkable scenario explains a lot about how we came to be, but it certainly doesn't help the rocket scientists. Without vast antimatter fields sprinkled generously throughout the universe, we have no fuel source for our ships. While it is true we have made some in particle accelerators, the amounts have been pathetically small. Furthermore, antimatter is tough and expensive to produce, and once you make it, where do you store it? If you put it in a beaker, a test tube, a crate, a barrel, a closet, you will be sweeping up after the explosion. But the idea that a ship could be powered by such a perfect fuel was too tempting to pass up. As early as 1953— before the antiproton was even found—the dreamers were at their drafting tables.

The first design came from the German rocket engineer Eugen Sänger who proposed combining electrons and positrons at regularly spaced intervals to produce a beam of energy. In theory it sounded pretty good, but there were problems. When an electron and positron collide, they are changed into gamma rays. Now, the gamma rays are very energetic and travel at superhigh speeds—which is good— but this makes them hard to stop. They can easily penetrate all kinds of materials, not least of which is the human cell where they can disrupt the genetic structure. So gamma radiation becomes extremely dangerous to the crew, and any ship with this stuff pouring out its tail end would have to be heavily shielded with lead. This would probably be okay as long as we could be guaranteed a narrow, highly concentrated gamma ray beam, but a beam is a very tall order.

Gamma rays are even less dependable than the weather. It's impossible to predict which way they'll be moving when they pop into existence. They can streak off at any angle, tricky enough when there are only two of them. But a ship with an antimatter drive will have to contend with hundreds of billions of high-speed gamma rays tearing away in all directions. And this is frighteningly similar to what happens when a nuclear bomb explodes—lots of gamma radiation suddenly unleashed in what amounts to a free-for-all.

In addition to posing a serious threat to the passengers inside, a large percentage of this explosive energy will be lost. Rather than being channeled into a nice, tight, powerful beam, the radiation will be spread out all over the place. It might look pretty spectacular, but it wouldn't have enough oomph to drive the ship.

For a while, Sänger tried to work through the problem. He fiddled around with various ideas for a gamma ray funnel that would redirect and focus the energy, but nothing seemed to have much potential. At last he admitted defeat and abandoned the whole design. The gamma rays had won.

Sometimes being the first puts you at a disadvantage. Sänger was so futuristic in his thinking, he even beat the science fiction writers, but as things turned out, he was a little too fast. When Sänger proposed his annihilation starship, he had only one kind of antiparticle to work with—the positron. But if he had waited for the antiproton to show up, he might have had something.

Just as protons, neutrons, and electrons have different and distinct characteristics, so do their corresponding antiparticles. Imagine three fruit pairs: a red grape and a green grape;

a peach and a nectarine; and a cantaloupe and a honeydew. Notice that the fruits in each pair are similar—the cantaloupe and honeydew are both melons, for instance—but they are not interchangeable.

We can use the fruits to simulate particle/antiparticle annihilation by squashing them together. If we squash the two grapes we get grape juice. But if we squash the peach and nectarine, we don't get grape juice. We get, instead, "peacharine" juice, and when we do the same with the cantaloupe and honeydew, we come out with yet a third kind of juice. Three different fruit pairs, three different juices.

The same is true for particles and antiparticles. Each pair produces different kinds of energy. So if a particle physicist, let's say, didn't happen to like grape juice, he or she could always smash some other kind of fruit.

Sänger knew that an electron/positron annihilation would produce gamma rays (and massless neutrinos, but they don't count). But what he did not know was that a proton and antiproton smashup would yield something scientists call pi-mesons, or pions for short. And pions we can work with.

It is a fact of nature that pions don't live very long. They quickly turn into gamma rays and neutrinos. *But . . .* not that quickly, and while they are still pions, they can be directed out the exhaust chamber in a tight beam. So who cares if they decay into gamma rays a moment later? They've already provided the necessary thrust. And as an extra added attraction, when the gamma rays pop into existence, they've already been left far behind the ship.

Great! What are we waiting for? Let's start building!

Well, what we are waiting for is the antimatter. There isn't any, remember? Oh sure, a few positrons here, a couple of antiprotons there, but certainly nothing like what we would need to fuel an interstellar ship. So until we find the antimatter equivalent of the Comstock Lode in space, we are not going to get off the ground with pions.

By the way, in case you happen to be wondering how we would store this potentially explosive stuff inside the ship, don't give it another thought. Engineers feel confident that they have worked it all out. The particles, of course, are no problem. They would be segregated from the antiparticles and held in a fuel sphere. The antiparticles would also be held in a fuel sphere, but one whose sides they would not be allowed to touch since the sphere would be made of ordinary matter. Furthermore, the sphere would have to be a vacuum. Air, like everything else, consists of atoms—oxygen, nitrogen, and various trace gases. Atoms are made of elementary particles, and elementary particles are not the kinds of things we want hanging around antiparticles. So the air gets pumped out, and the fuel is kept suspended in the center of the sphere by means of a powerful magnetic field. But before you rush out and organize an antimatter search party, consider this:

When protons and antiprotons annihilate each other, not all the energy they produce is usable. Actually, most of the stuff goes out with the trash. Nearly half is in the form of neutrinos. Remember them? The good-for-nothings who can't sit still? Neutrinos also refuse to be coaxed, threatened, cajoled, forced, or sweet-talked into a narrow beam. Nothing—not even powerful magnetic fields—has any effect on them. So subtract neutrinos from the total starship thrust.

There are also various pion forms produced in the explosion. Some have a positive charge, some a negative charge, and some are neutral. The neutral pions we can forget about. They "decay" into gamma rays almost at once and are completely worthless. Only the charged pions can be herded into a beam to help move our starship along, but unfortunately, they are way down in the percentages. So when all is said and done and we are going full tilt, our final velocity in an annihilation-powered starship is just 30 percent light speed.

What! All that hard work for a measly 55,800 miles per second? Forget it! Call off the antimatter search party. We'll use something else, something really fast that can be channeled into a beam, a light-speed beam, a . . .

A beam of light!

Enter the photon rocket, a starship that runs on the very stuff that gave light speed its name. A starship whose exhaust velocity would be the ultimate—186,282 miles per second—and whose wake would be a glittering trail of light beams, like a brilliant golden streak in the everblack of space.

Wow!

Of all the starship designs, the photon rocket is certainly the most beautiful. It is also the least likely to succeed, but for the moment, let's not talk about the bad stuff.

A photon (from a word meaning "light unit") is a tiny packet of electromagnetic energy. We call this particular kind of energy light, and it pours as easily from our desk lamp as it does from quasars.

Photons are emitted in little bursts whenever an atom "downshifts" to a lower energy state. We can number an atom's energy levels from 1 to 10, where 1 is very calm and 10 is extremely excited. If the atom is at level 10 and suddenly drops to level 9, a photon shoots out. This is how the atom pays for changing its energy level. Cost: one photon.

Now, the photon tears off at the speed of light cleverly disguised as a wave. Light waves are energy transport systems. If the wave happens to run into another atom, and if it hits the atom squarely in the right place, it can transfer its little bit of energy to the new atom. That way, nothing is ever lost. What one atom gives up, another atom receives.

Since photons do indeed carry energy (which is really another form of mass), and since they hustle along at light speed, they seem like perfect candidates to power starships. They appear to have the two characteristics of a good rocket fuel—exhaust mass and exhaust velocity. When we multiply them together we get thrust, and thrust, as you know, nudges ships along through the interstellar void. But if you are really keeping your eyes peeled, you have probably spotted the fly in the ointment.

Here's a hint. How much exhaust mass can photons really have? Think about it. Every minute of every day photons are streaming out of table lamps, flashlights, floodlights at baseball stadiums, taillights and high beams of cars, the bulbs inside refrigerators, and yet, *none of these things ever goes anywhere!* Clyde Leadfoot turns on the headlights of his car and does not career backward down Main Street. At dusk, the streetlights in your town go on, but they do not shoot upward, break free of Earth's gravitational pull, and head off into outer space. In fact, everything—no exceptions—that emits photons stays put. Everything. Rockets included.

Yes, photons are fast. The best exhaust velocity in all the universe. And yes, photons carry energy that can be translated into exhaust mass, but the amount of mass is extremely tiny. In short, a light bulb has no thrust, and a photon rocket wouldn't have any either.

And so, as the sun sets on Chapter 6, we are still without a decent interstellar ship. But don't worry, because there's always science fiction to fall back on. So kindly step this way to Chapter 7. . . . ★

CHAPTER 7

★

Science Fiction Fun

We could be halfway across the galaxy by now if it weren't for those miserable rules. You know the ones—the action/reaction thing, Einstein's business with the speed of light, all that gravity stuff. . . . It's enough to drive a rocket engineer deep into the caverns of the science fiction section of the library, because there, the impossible in science becomes intriguingly, tantalizingly possible. Particle physics takes a holiday, and Einstein takes a hike. Away we go into outer space in a ship with no moving parts.

Travel to the stars is child's play if you have a word processor and a friendly publisher. Writers have always found it astonishingly easy to go anywhere their plots required. They have jumped through black holes, popped into hyperspace with their annihilation engines, and, since the dawn of the printing press almost, raised their antigravity shields and shot away.

Antigravity is one of science fiction's most beloved devices. Despite its super farfetched no-one-is-going-to-believe-it nature, antigravity slips in and out of novels and stories with a comfortable familiarity. You can hardly get from *Gulliver's Travels,* written in the eighteenth century, to modern-day James Blish's *Cities in Flight* without encountering some form of the antigravity machine.

Antigravity operates on the principle of opposites: gravity attracts; antigravity repels. Launching our spacecraft from the ultradense planet Bonga-Bonga in the star system Razz 4 is so very difficult because of gravity. But activate those antigravity shields and up we go.

What's that? You see a nifty planet out the starboard window? You'd like to land and maybe visit a few of the sites? Sure thing. Easy as pi. We just throw this switch and adjust this lever, and the antigravity shields smoothly fold up. Now we drift, and when our ship gets close enough to the nifty planet, it is attracted by the planet's gravity and presto! We land.

Wow! Some stuff this antigravity is. And it doesn't even use fuel.

But seriously, how come there is no such thing as antigravity? Why is it in the forbidden zone?

Let's begin at the beginning with Sir Isaac Newton and his mother's apple trees. According to the story, one afternoon Newton just happened to see an apple tumble out of a tree and hit the ground with a wallop. Chances are, Newton had seen things fall plenty of times before, but this time the lightning bolt of inspiration struck him squarely between the frontal lobes.

"I wonder," he said, "if this apple drop has anything in common with the moon. . . . Funny how the moon just hangs up there when it should want to fly off into space. Could it be that Earth's gravity is holding on to it?"

Newton's famous interlude in the apple orchard gave us the theory that gravity is a force somehow generated by massive objects such as the Earth. This force of gravity draws things toward the object's center, although it seems to weaken as the objects move away from each other. That would mean distance affects the pull of gravity on an object. So a roving asteroid, for instance, could be captured by a planet if it strayed too close, if it entered the planet's gravitational "field."

Newton's theory of gravity was simple and elegant, but it never really explained what gravity is. It almost sounded as if gravity were some sort of emanation, like the zigzag rays that shoot out of a cartoon magician's fingers when he casts a spell. Of course, there was nothing wrong with zigzag rays as long as we could think up a source for them. Was something disintegrating? Leaking? Exploding? Decaying? Was gravity even zigzag rays at all?

If gravity had turned out to be rays (it isn't), physics would be in a fine mess, but the antigravity machine industry probably would have flourished. A little imagination and at least ten manufacturers would have come up with an all-purpose shield, guaranteed to block out gravity for fifty years or your money back.

Fortunately, along came Einstein.

In 1915, Einstein published his general theory of relativity. In it he presented a strikingly original view of gravity that totally eclipsed Newton's simple ideas. Relativity doesn't show that Newton was wrong; he just wasn't detailed enough. We understand gravity today because of both of these great scientists, so don't throw away your Newton decoder ring.

According to Einstein (as you no doubt recall from Chapter 1), all objects make gravitational dents in space, much the way a three-hundred-pound weight lifter would make a dent in the jumping bed of a trampoline if he were to stand on it. If we set a teddy bear on the jumping bed, it will tumble inward toward the weight lifter because it is affected by his gravitational dent.

Since everything, regardless of its size, dents space, the biggest of the big and the smallest of the small can be both an attractor and an attractee. The strength of the attraction depends only on the object's mass. You, for example, attract the Earth just as the Earth attracts you, but not enough to be "felt" by the planet. That's why when you execute a cannonball into a swimming pool, you're the one who falls downward; the planet doesn't spring up toward you. The gravity well you create isn't as deep as the one made by the Earth.

Gravity can almost be described as a situation rather than a mysterious force or pull. You could actually see it on a three-dimensional map of outer space. If the stars, planets, nebulae, and various bits of space junk were represented as spheres, each and every one would be sitting within a depression. Just as lakes and mountains are part of the topography of the Earth, gravity is part of the topography of space. So the old-fashioned term "gravitational field" still applies. The only problem is that a lot of people start thinking that a gravitational field is just like a magnetic field when it's not even close.

Max Gummy, owner of We Mush 'Em, a car junkyard, has a giant compactor that transforms old '61 Chevys with their engines torn out into little metallic cubes. But the mouth of the compactor is at least fifteen feet off the ground, so Max uses a huge electromagnet to lift the cars up. Max throws a switch that turns on a current of electricity. The electricity flows into a giant iron disk and causes the iron atoms to realign themselves. This realignment turns the iron into a magnet.

Max then works the controls and slowly moves the electromagnet over to one of his car victims, a '53 Buick that has seen better days. As the magnet nears the Buick, the car's metallic roof starts to feel the effects of the magnetic field. In a moment it is all over. The Buick has been drawn to the magnet, and—to the delight of Miss Thornrose's second-grade class, which happens to be on a gravitational field trip—the Buick now dangles high above the junkyard.

Now, here's where magnetic fields have gravitational fields beat by a mile. To release the Buick from the magnet, all Max has to do is flip the switch and kill the electric current flowing into the iron. The atoms in the iron will return to their original unmagnetized state, and the car will drop like a ton of . . . er, metal. But because gravitational fields are created by the warping of space, there is no way to turn them off. In order for an antigravity machine to work, it would have to *unwarp* space.

Buster Bohinkus, Max's shady competitor from Crushing Is Us, knows another way to knock out a magnetic field. He can put a lead shield on the roof of each car. Lead is one metal not affected by magnetic fields, so it can act as a barrier. But what could you use as a barrier against gravity? If feeling the effects of gravity is like tumbling into a well, how do we keep our rocket ship out of the well? Build some sort of cosmic plank? The plank will be drawn in. Unlike lead, glass, and a whole bunch of other materials that are not the least bit fazed by magnetic fields, everything, *everything!* falls victim to the ultimate master of the universe—gravity.

All right, so we can't use shields, but what about trying to unwarp space? Is there some way to make space stiffer so it doesn't sag so much? Not as far as we know.

Another idea—equally as far out—is to reverse the curvature of space by turning the gravity dents inside out so they lead away from the object. But even Flash Gordon, yelling advice from the twenty-fifth century, says pass on this one. To invert a gravity dent, Flash says, we would need negative mass, and negative mass doesn't exist—at least scientists are pretty sure it doesn't exist. If it did, though, it would be less than nothing. It would have minus mass. If you put it on a scale, the pound counter would roll backward, past zero. Negative mass would unweigh. And it would create the opposite of a dent in the fabric of space: It would create a bubble.

But wait. It gets goofier. One of Newton's famous equations (even though you may never have heard of it) is $F = ma$. $F = ma$ is Newton's second law of motion, the one that Clyde Leadfoot and other stranded motorists are likely to know all about. Basically, it says that a big, fat, heavy car that has run out of gas is harder to push than a plywood go-cart.

Newton's equation also says that you'd better be in shape when you start pushing that stalled car because the more massive the object, the more force you need to get it moving. And don't expect too much in the way of acceleration, either. Massive objects are hard to speed up.

Oh . . . and one more thing. Newton's equation advises you to decide which way you want to go before you start pushing the car. That's because the direction of the force determines the direction of travel. So if you are planning to head south toward Buddy's Gas Emporium, push in a southward direction.

And there you have F = ma. Logical, isn't it? But suppose we make a little substitution. Instead of using positive mass like a car, let's use negative mass. Here's what happens to the equation: F = (negative) ma. Even if you're not a math whiz, you still know what "equals" means, and in this new equation it means trouble. Before, if we pushed the car in a southward direction, it headed south. But now, using a car that has negative mass, if we push in a southward direction, the car moves the opposite way! It heads north, toward us! And the harder we push, the worse it gets until we are run over by our own car!

So we have been too smart for our own good. In our at-

Sir Isaac Newton formulated the equation that makes Clyde Leadfoot's stalled car so hard to move.

tempt to invert gravity wells with negative mass, we have made the attraction even stronger. The more force we use to lift our spaceship off the Earth, the faster it accelerates in the opposite direction—toward the Earth! No wonder Flash Gordon didn't want any part of this.

So despite our wildest, most energetic efforts, the score is still, science: 1, antigravity: 0. But before we leave this beloved device to the likes of Jules Verne, one final remark. Even if most of the rules of physics suddenly took a nosedive out the window and antigravity became possible, we still wouldn't have such a wonderful thing. You have already seen that a slow, leisurely Sunday drive across space is not recommended. The universe is vast, and a human life span is woefully short. So all our efforts have been aimed at speeding up the ship, pushing it as fast as we can possibly get it to go. Or, as they say in the cartoons, we have to make our ship go *varoooo-o-o-o-ooom!*

An antigravity machine—even the deluxe model—is basically just a shield. It's passive. It won't make our ship move under its own power because it doesn't provide any thrust. Furthermore, an antigravity device is absolutely dependent on the presence of a gravitational field. Sure, we could launch our ship quite efficiently from a massive planet. But suppose we were moving through space at, say, 50 percent light speed and we wanted to increase our velocity. Suppose we wanted to accelerate. We couldn't do it. If there's no nearby massive object, we can never go any faster than our original "repulsion velocity."*

---

*This made-up term refers to the speed at which a ship would be repelled by an object such as a star or planet. Since more massive objects have stronger gravitational pulls, it stands to reason that they would also have higher repulsion velocities when their gravity is blocked. So the stronger the repulsion, the higher the velocity.

But if you're interested in something along the lines of, say, instantaneous travel, and if your imagination is still running, there's another option. It's called matter transmission. Perhaps you've heard of it.

It is Thursday, June 24. At 7:14 A.M. you are sitting at the kitchen table casually shoveling Rice Chex and bananas into your mouth. At 7:18 you finish breakfast, put your bowl and spoon into the dishwasher, and yell, "Bye, Ma!" to which Ma replies, "Have a nice day, dear!"

At 7:19 you step out onto the back porch and flip open your communicator. "Testing . . . ," you say, and then, "Er . . . could you beam me up, Scotty, please?"

It is 7:19:01. Your atoms have been disassembled, channeled into a thin beam, shot through the universe at speeds that would make Einstein's hair frizz, and reassembled, letter-perfect, on the cool, blue shores of Lake Metho-Metho in the Googolplex Galaxy.

"Welcome to Planet 5-B," says Scotty, handing you a helmet and a life-support system. "Enjoy your trip?"

If nature allowed us to choose one device from science fiction, it might very well be the matter transmitter. Unlike the antigravity machine, which is just a little too conservative for most people's tastes, the matter transmitter is good old-fashioned space fun. The control panel, as we all know from watching Captain Kirk on "Star Trek," is no bigger than a Crayola eight-pack. Maybe you can only take carry-on luggage, but with long-distance travel this easy, who needs to stay overnight? Best of all, though, is the matter transmitter's range. It is virtually limitless. And since the matter transmitter apparently defies all the rules of Einsteinian speed, you can be in orbit around the most distant quasar in the blink of an eye. Wow! Could things get any better?

Well, yes. The matter transmitter could be a lot better if it were even remotely possible. But unfortunately, this wonderful, imaginative device assumes that the computer—its single most important component—is mightier than it can ever be. Sure, computers can play chess. They can launch spacecraft and make course corrections. They can speculate on how the universe might have formed. But they cannot—and will never be able to—reassemble a human being from a pile of binary data. They couldn't even make a fly.

In 1958 actor David Hedison scared us all half to death in the science fiction film *The Fly*. In it, Hedison is a brilliant if slightly misguided scientist who has built a matter transmitter. Anxious to try it out, Hedison steps inside, closes the door, and flips the switch. The device works, but there is a rather nasty accident.

Hedison isn't alone when he enters the transmitter. He unknowingly shares the chamber with a fly whose atoms become scrambled with Hedison's during reassembly. Hedison emerges with the fly's head, and the fly winds up with Hedison's head, proportional in size, by the way. Pretty ugly stuff.

As we sat among the empty Jujube boxes in the darkened theater, the warm, buttery scent of popcorn hanging heavy in the air, we shouted advice to David Hedison.

"Why don't you look for the fly?" we screamed. (We figured he had to know there was a fly walking around somewhere with his head.) "Find the fly," we urged, "and get back into that stupid transmitter!"

We were pretty naive. We mistakenly assumed that a second disassembling and reassembling would put things right. Hedison and the fly would get their own heads back. But despite the fact that the mix-up looked neat, it had really been random. The matter transmitter had reduced the scientist and the fly to their individual genetic components. In transit, these components had gotten mixed together and upon reassembly, some fly stuff had gotten into the human stuff. Had Hedison and the fly returned to the transmitter for another shot at it, the same breakdown would have occurred, but certainly not the same scrambling of parts. In fact, there are an almost infinite number of ways Hedison and the fly could have been reassembled. A second transmission might have made things better, but it could also have made things considerably worse. To get his own head back, Hedison would have had to be prepared to undergo billions and billions of transmissions. And after about ten thousand years, the laws of probability may have paid off—or then again, maybe not. It was, as you see, a very nasty lab accident.

If we can learn anything from David Hedison's misadventure, it is never to enter a matter transmitter with another living being. But even if we make the journey alone, and, just to be on the safe side, remove watches, rings, glasses, false teeth, and clothes, we've still got problems. And the problems lie, as usual, with the speed of light, according to which a *real* transmitter would have to operate.

A matter transmitter is essentially a delivery service. Information is physically moved from Point A to Point B; not duplicated, as with a Xerox machine, but transferred. A matter transmitter sends information in the form of a beam. The beam consists of elementary particles that travel at the speed of light, and since the particles are the package, Einsteinian delivery is guaranteed.

"Lemme tell you about our breakdown operation," says Warren LeGlue, head salesman for Zi-i-i-p! Matter Transmitter Company, and from the depths of his imitation leather attaché case, he produces a small brochure.

Before transmission, the package must first be broken down into tiny, transportable bits that can be focused into a beam.

"If we didn't do this," Warren interrupts, "funny relativity stuff would happen."

"Like what?" you want to know.

Warren explains that as an object approaches the speed of light, it becomes more and more massive. At light speed, the object's mass is infinite.

"Er . . . but that's impossible," you say.

"Exactly," replies Warren, "which is why we have to trick Einstein and disguise the package. We break the package down into its most elementary particles, the ones that not only can travel at light speed, but *have to!* We aim the beam in the desired direction, and through a process that is both secret and totally science fictional, the object re-forms upon arrival."

"Wow!" you say, because of course you are very impressed.

Now, you are just about to sign on the dotted line for a little trip across the solar system when you are suddenly struck by the questionable safety of the dismantling end of things. You remember a toy once that came in a box with the warning SOME ASSEMBLY REQUIRED. What a nightmare!

"Excuse me, Mr. LeGlue . . . ," you say.

"Call me Warren." He grins expansively.

But you don't feel like grinning back. You are worried. What if the matter transmitter can't reassemble you on the other end? What if it gets your parts mixed up? You mention the stories about a truck that was sent to one of Jupiter's moons and when it arrived, its front tires were where the rear tires should have been.

"Aw, no harm done," replies Warren, removing the cap of his pen so you can sign on the dotted line. "People rotate their tires all the time."

You gasp. "But what if the matter transmitter rotates my arms and legs? Forget it! I'm not going! It's much too risky."

"It's true, Zi-i-i-p! hasn't worked out all the bugs yet, but . . ."

Now you are really quaking in your boots. Bugs. Ugh! What was the name of that movie, again?

A matter transmitter would be useless to anyone except a scoundrelly space villain if it couldn't guarantee a perfect reassembly. As the particle information spills from the exit pipe of the machine, something must govern its rearrangement. A jigsaw puzzle may have as many as 10,000 pieces, but there is only one way to put the puzzle together, and it has nothing whatsoever to do with the picture. The arrangement of the pieces depends solely on their shapes and the way they fit into each other. So you can assemble the puzzle even if you don't know what the picture is (although it will probably take a lot longer).

Fortunately for future matter transmitter manufacturers, all living things come with a highly detailed set of blueprints. It is our genetic code, our DNA. Within each cell of our body can be found the DNA double helix, two gently curling strands of complex acids and proteins. The strands are joined throughout their length by barlike structures, giving the whole thing the appearance of a twisted rope ladder. All that is you lies coded in your DNA. It is the ultimate recipe, an accurate and elegant plan for building—or rebuilding—you and you alone. Your DNA knows not only what size and shape your nose should be, but where it goes.

"Perfect!" shouts Lynda May Meegle, owner and chairperson of the board of Zi-i-i-p! Matter Transmitters.

Suddenly, she has seen the light, and it has all come clear to her. From this day forward, all matter transmission travelers will be broken down into their basic genetic components. They will be dismantled gene by gene, and the DNA information will be beamed across the vast reaches of time and space. And in a grand and majestic finale, the voyager will reassemble in fine precision on the distant shores of Andromeda.

It must be pointed out, however, that in real life and real time, we are not even close to a complete genetic mapping of ourselves. While it is true that scientists have discovered a handful of what they call genetic markers, they are still far from anything even remotely resembling a picture. So, although Lynda May has a good idea, it is an idea whose time has not yet come. But let's humor her a little.

A massive computer is now dragged onto the scene and hooked up to a matter transmitter. You are invited to KINDLY STEP THIS WAY → and make yourself comfortable inside.

"Ready?" Lynda May asks.

"Ready whenever you are," you reply with a wink.

Lynda May throws the switch, and quick as that wink you just made, the computer begins to process your DNA profile. Now we wait.

And wait.

And wait.

Bit by bit, the data is absorbed by the computer and translated into ones and zeros—the binary code. The computer works nonstop, all day and all night, processing this information at the speed of light. But still we must wait. There is a lot of information. There are teeny, tiny details about the texture of your skin, the thickness of your cranial nerves, the shape of the nuclei in your white blood cells. Exactly how many rods and cones will be in your eyeballs? Will you be allergic to pollen? Will you get diabetes? How long will it take your biceps to fatigue when you lift weights? How fast will you be able to run?

And on and on and on and on and on . . .

Ten years pass, and still your genetic profile remains incomplete. Twenty years. A hundred. The computer hums on through the nights sprinkled silver with stars. The planets dance overhead in their orbits. Pluto makes one complete voyage around the sun. We wait. So much information . . .

As long as the light limit determines the speed at which information can be sent, matter transmission will remain a very slow way to travel. And because of some rather obvious technical difficulties, it will also remain beyond the reality fringe. But perhaps some things should stay forever outside our grasp. Then there will always be something to reach for, and we can keep on dreaming and having science fiction fun. ★

CHAPTER 8

★

Albert's Magic

*T*he Great Alberto stepped slowly up to the blackboard. *T*, he wrote with a sweeping flourish, and the audience held its collective breath.

"It's from relativity," someone whispered.

His blue eyes twinkling playfully, the Great Alberto added an "equals" sign and then a strange hieroglyphic, which he said represented a square root.

"Oh!" gasped a woman in the fourth row who had already guessed the trick. She clutched the sides of her folding chair and prepared for the fabulous trip through time.

The Great Alberto scribbled a few more magic marks on the blackboard with his chalk wand and, turning to the audience, shouted, "Presto-o-o-o-o change-o-o!" in German.

And in that moment, everyone saw the amazing mathematical trick. There it was, written on a blackboard in tall letters and curious symbols, pointing the way to the stars.

It could give the travelers the precious time they needed to see all the places they had dreamed about . . . the star clusters and nebulae, the faraway planets drifting silently through the spacedark. . . . And the galaxies, especially the galaxies, turning like carnival pinwheels, a billion light-years away. Yes, there it was for all to see. The thing they call the time dilation effect. A little bit of Albert's magic.

Unless you were an aging beauty queen, you didn't give much thought to time before Einstein. It simply was. It flowed ever forward like a vast, unchanging river, carrying all things with it, from protozoa to galaxies. But it was this somewhat dull image of time that allowed legions of science fiction writers to build time-travel machines for their intrepid heroes. As long as time was a body of water with a one-way current, all a writer had to do was devise some suitable futuristic container and ship his or her characters upstream. What could be simpler? But then along came Einstein with his new and improved concept of time, and in one stroke, the ferryboat operators were out of business.

Einstein's relativity equations seemed to be suggesting that instead of a river, time was probably more like a rubber band. While this isn't exactly what you might call poetic, it does open up a lot of interesting possibilities. For instance, under the right conditions, time can be made to stretch, rather like the elastic band that holds up your sweatpants. Strange? Wait. You ain't heard nothin' yet.

Picture the seconds of existence marked off as black dots along the elastic band. When the band is stretched, the dots spread out and become more oval-shaped.* Now, if you were

---

*Hold it. You don't have to picture this. Just take an ordinary rubber band—the thicker, the better—and draw a row of dots on it with a marking pen. Then stretch the band. Notice what happens to the dots.

a little bacterium walking along the band you would start to notice something peculiar. The more the band is stretched, the longer it takes you to cover the distance across one dot. Since each dot represents a second, the seconds have essentially gotten "longer." Time has slowed down.

The benefits of this so-called time dilation (the word *dilation* means "to widen") are pretty obvious. If time is slowing down, you must be aging more slowly. If you're aging more slowly, you can set out for very faraway places and know that you will live long enough to reach them.

*A*lbert Einstein, *who not only changed a few rules, but taught us some daring new ones*

AIP, NIELS BOHR LIBRARY

With the effects of time dilation pushed to their absolute limit, you can tour the 250 stars that make up the Pleiades cluster, 410 light-years away. Or, if you prefer something a little less cluttered, you can visit the wispy Trifid nebula, 5,200 light-years away. Looking for a real adventure? Amazing but true: Time dilation will actually allow you to cross the Milky Way and enter the borders of the great galaxy in Andromeda, 2.2 million light-years from Earth. Thanks to Einstein, we really can travel to the stars.

There is, however, one condition that must be met first. In order to get time to dilate, we have to be moving very, very fast. Speed is the single factor that makes the whole thing work, but it is hard to achieve. Our best rocket designs can give us perhaps 35 percent to 40 percent light speed, and that's not enough. Only at speeds in excess of 90 percent c* do the strange effects of time dilation begin to kick in. And the faster the ship moves, the slower time moves, until at light speed precisely, time stands still.

Without a doubt, this dilation business is good news for long-distance spacefarers, but only if they don't plan on returning home. Time dilation is limited exclusively to the passengers on board the speeding ship. Back on Earth, time marches along at its normal pace, so the faster and further the space travelers go, the more they separate themselves from the folks they left behind. If at some point they decide to turn the ship around and head back, they will get the shock of their dilated lives. Blame it on the Einstein factor.

As the ship accelerates beyond 167,650 miles per second,† the Einstein factor increases from 1 to 2. For every one month

---

*c is the mathematical abbreviation for light speed, as in Einstein's $E = mc^2$.

†This velocity is 90 percent light speed based on c = 186,282 miles per second.

that passes on the ship, two months elapse on the Earth. One year ship time equals two years Earth time. Not so bad, you say, but it's unlikely a deep space ship will stay at 90 percent light speed. So let's boost it up to 184,420 miles per second, or 99 percent c. At this velocity the Einstein Factor becomes 7. One ship-year is now equivalent to seven Earth-years, and that's when things start to get uncomfortable.

You are a thirteen-year-old passenger of the starship *Albert Einstein*. After using up one Earth-year to accelerate to 99 percent light speed, the *Albert Einstein* heads out on a seven-year ship-time journey to the far distant planet Zignor 5. The ship then swings around and heads home. Add another seven ship-years for the return trip and one Earth-year for deceleration. Total elapsed time for you: sixteen years. You are now twenty-nine.

Meanwhile, back at the ranch, your younger (and very bratty) brother Elmer, who was nine when you left, is having a rather tough go of it. Not only has his hair fallen out completely—except for one pesky strand—but his walker has the most annoying wobble. Little Elmer, cute, bothersome little Elmer, is about to celebrate his hundred-and-ninth birthday! The fourteen ship-years for you turned into fourteen times seven, or ninety-eight years for Elmer. (You each get two "regular" years for acceleration and deceleration.)

But shocking as this may be, you should count your blessings. As a spaceship inches closer and closer toward the magic speed limit, time dilates to wild extremes. At 99.999 percent light speed—just two miles a second short of c—you would be able to cross the Milky Way and actually enter the Andromeda galaxy, over 2 million light-years away. But the price of admission is high, and it may turn out to be too high for most people. While the space-time voyager would rack up only about 15 years (counting one year to accelerate), Earth would have aged 2.2 *million* years! You could never go home.

And what would life be like inside a ship where time is crawling along on its belly?

Glad you asked.

Suppose we haul out the Acme Optics Company's Ultra-Modified Superman See-Through Telescope and have a look.

"Hey!" you cry. "What is this, some kind of trick? There's nothing happening inside that spaceship! Everybody's frozen stuck!"

Keep looking.

"I am looking, but I don't . . . oops, wait a minute . . . wait just a minute . . . I think I see something. Wow! The passengers are all moving around in slow motion! V-e-r-y slow motion. That must be weird."

Well, actually, the passengers don't even notice it. Ultra high speeds and the elasticity of time combine to create a totally separate reality for them. At 99.9 percent light speed, the ship has become a little world unto itself. Nobody can tell that time has slowed down because everything in, around, and on the ship is affected. The very atoms of which the passengers are made are actually moving more slowly. The neurons in their brains are firing more slowly. They're breathing, reacting, even thinking more slowly, so how can they possibly know that anything has changed? It's the perfect "illusion."

But you and all the rest of us back home are not part of the relativity trick. For us, time is just slip-sliding along at its "normal" pace, so from our vantage point, everybody on the ship looks as if they are moving in slow motion.

So which is the fake reality and which is the real one? You should already know the answer. It's all relative.

A spaceship moving very close to light speed is full of surprises. In addition to time dilation, two other rather oddball effects begin to show up. They are length contraction and mass increase, and once again, the passengers are completely oblivious to the fact that things have run amok.

Length contraction is pretty much what it sounds like; as the ship accelerates, it appears to get shorter. The amount of contraction, of course, depends on the speed of the ship. At 60 percent light speed, the ship's length is reduced by about 20 percent, meaning that a ship measuring twenty city blocks (one mile) when it was launched now looks as if it is only sixteen blocks long. Not bad, you say, but a true interstellar ship can hardly be expected to go poking through the universe at a mere 111,600 miles per second. So let's crank up the engines to something a little more respectable.

We now find ourselves at 99.9 percent light speed, and according to the shrinking formula, called a Lorentz transformation, the mile-long vehicle appears to have shrunk to just over 237 feet—about 20 yards shorter than a football field.

"Oh, no!" you cry. "Those poor passengers, all squashed together like that!"

But our intrepid space voyagers are in no such predicament. Since the contents of the ship are also moving at 99.9 percent light speed, they too are contracting in length, so on board, no one's the wiser.

At the very same time, however, the mass of the ship is *increasing,* and if we could somehow weigh the ship we would find that it is topping the scales at more than 22 times its "rest" weight. And the passengers and crew naturally follow suit. Thanks to the wonder of relativity, Irma Fitzrumple, in stateroom 9B, now weighs something close to the average midsize car (fully equipped).

Gosh, can things get any worse for the poor passengers?

Yes. As the velocity rises toward 186,282 miles per second, the conditions inside the ship will become more and more extreme until, engines gasping, the ship is held by the light-speed barrier.

It is now appropriate to ask why the ship can't achieve light speed.

Well consider this: At light speed three things ought to happen. First, time will stand dead still. Second, the ship's mass will be infinite. And finally, the ship will completely disappear because it will have shrunk up to nothing.

"Oh, ho!" you exclaim, your eyes popping wide in delight. "Wouldn't that be something to see!"

The scientists certainly think so. Who wouldn't want to see three completely impossible conditions occurring at the same time? But even though the math says yes, the physics says no. As the ship inches closer and closer to light speed, it grows more massive, and, as you learned way back in Chapter 1, the more massive the ship, the more fuel is required to accelerate it. To nudge the ship up to light speed exactly, we would need an infinite amount of fuel since the ship would then be infinitely massive. And that is why a spaceship can never reach or accelerate past the speed of light.

Still, 99.999 percent light speed is plenty fast enough for our needs. In twenty-five ship-years you could be 10 billion light-years from Earth, and that is awfully far. The most distant galaxy ever found is 15 billion light-years away, almost at the edge of the known universe. Conceivably, if the captain were to turn the ship around and head home without stopping, the entire astonishing trip would take just fifty ship-years. But sadly, you would not be greeted by cheering crowds anxious to hear of your great journey across space and time. You would not silently cruise into a friendly blue-

and-white home port where grass grows and water renews the land. Ten billion years is a long time, far longer than our solar system can survive.

As the ship makes its way back through millennial space, the sun will already have swollen grotesquely. Its original fuel sources used up, it will begin to feed off the heavier elements it has made. For a time, the sun will blaze like never before, but there will be no one left on Earth to see the spectacular closing act. First Mercury and then Venus and Earth will be swallowed up in the sun's expanding gas layers. Mars will be a cinder. And Pluto, once terrifyingly cold, could be warm enough to support a small human outpost. But after 10 billion years of evolution, of civilizations rising and falling and perhaps crumbling forever into dust, will there be any people left at all?

The near-light-speed sailor will have to be tough, a mariner from the old school, willing to forsake friends and family and all things secure for a one-way ride through time. The years before planetfall will be long and monotonous, occupied with ship's chores, petty daily routines, and limited recreation. The corridors, made cheerful by high technology, will cross and recross through the three-quarter-mile vehicle and never lead anywhere. For eight hours in every twenty-four, the lights will dim to simulate night, an attempt to preserve some of the old ways of Earth. But the black nothing outside, star specked and eternally cold, will reveal the truth.

Certainly, a star mariner's life will be emotionally hard. Marriages will inevitably occur, but they will bring with them strict birth limitations. The living quarters will be comfortable and the food, homegrown and good; but the ship will always remain a tender prison from which there can be no escape. Burials will be solemn, almost peaceful, as the dead are returned to the all-embracing stars, but each passing will take something of a lost Earth with it. And so, the journey will be for the tough ones, the ones blinded by the stardust they would pay any price to see.

But there is something more, something that the universe offers only to those brave enough to sail on the edge of light speed. It is reserved for the sailors on board a Bussard ramjet perhaps, or a tomorrow ship with an antimatter drive. Some may call it a mirage, an optical illusion, a trick of physics. Perhaps it is. But for the passengers and crew who gave up everything, the final light show at near c is the payoff.

To understand what will happen to the stars as the spaceship approaches light speed, we have to go back to about 1840. It was then that Austrian physicist Christian Doppler decided it was high time somebody explained that business with train whistles. (He would deal with light later.)

Here's the scene:

You're standing at a grade crossing and the 9:14 goes roaring by (said Doppler). The engineer, in an attempt to warn cows and other slowpokes that a train is coming, sounds the whistle.

Get off the tracks! screams the whistle, and keeps on screaming until you wonder if perhaps the engineer has fallen asleep at the whistle switch. *And then all at once you notice it.* As the train approaches, the pitch of the whistle steadily rises, climbing to an ear-splitting shriek until, in a thunder of clanging metal, the train is past you and the whistle's pitch falls like a ton of bricks.

"Gosh! What was that?" you ask.

To which Dr. Doppler would proudly reply, "That's my shift. Want to know how it works?"

The Doppler shift is something you notice when a sound, such as a whistle, is moving faster than you are. Just like time dilation and length contraction, the Doppler shift depends on your point of reference. (Remember the incredible shrinking spaceship?) Since the engineer is on the train traveling at the same speed as the whistle, he hears only one pitch. But you and the cows hear a change. As the whistle approaches you, the pitch rises; as it recedes, the pitch falls. Why?

The whistle creates sound waves that spread out in all directions at the speed of 1,088 feet per second.* But because the whistle is mounted on the moving train, it too is moving. It is moving at the same speed as the train, say 90 miles an hour. So as the train roars down the tracks, it carries the whistle into its own sound waves at 90 miles an hour.

Now, you are standing at the grade crossing, and what you hear are sound waves starting to bunch up in front of the train. Suppose you dropped a stone into a lake very close to shore. The ripples would not be spread out evenly. The ones that move toward the center of the lake will be nice, concentric circles, but the ripples that head toward the shoreline will bunch up, resulting in little waves.

The pitch of a sound depends on how bunched up the waves are. This is called the wavelength. Bunched waves have short wavelengths, while stretched-out waves have long wavelengths. The shorter the wavelength, the higher the pitch. So when a train is heading toward you and the sound waves are bunching up, you hear a high-pitched whistle. When the train passes you and races off down the track, the sound waves have to cover a greater and greater distance to reach your ears. They become stretched out, and the whistle's pitch gets lower.

---

*Sound changes speed depending on the medium. Some mediums provide a very efficient ferry service. When sound travels through glass, for example, its speed is a staggering 19,690 feet per second. Compare that to its water speed— 4,938 feet per second. And the thinner the air, the slower the speed.

But how (you must certainly be wondering) is all this Doppler business going to work in a vacuum? We need air to carry sound waves, and interstellar space is not exactly famous for its high air content. Well, it just so happens that light can be Doppler shifted too, and if you thought the train thing was good, wait until you see what the Doppler shift does with color.

For the longest time, everyone just assumed that light traveled around town in the form of waves. After all, there were sound waves, so why not light waves? But then we learned that light is actually a steady, unbroken stream of energy packets. These packets, which the scientists christened photons, speed away from their source at 186,282 miles per second and don't stop until they are absorbed by something, such as a wall. Well, this sounded pretty good to the physicists, and so there the matter rested, although not for long. When Einstein took a look at the situations, he declared light to be a *wavicle*. Light is particles, yes, but it can sometimes act like a wave, hence the word *wavicle*, which Einstein invented to make himself perfectly clear.

Einstein's wavicle word never really caught on, but his theory did, and today light is considered to have a dual personality. Lucky thing, because it's those curious wave properties that allow light, just like sound, to be Doppler shifted.

The universe is disgorging energy. Pouring out from every conceivable direction are X rays and gamma rays, microwaves, radio waves, and, of course, visible light. This is the *electromagnetic spectrum* in all its glory, and if you didn't know better, you'd wonder how anybody could get any sleep with so much going on. But you do know better. You know that human beings have been designed to pick up only a very small segment of this energy. It is the narrow middle section called the *visible spectrum*. This is where the light is.

What allows us to see light and not any of the other energy forms is simply the design of the human eye. If the waves emitted by a source such as a star are just a little too long, the energy falls into the infrared zone and we can no longer see it. If the waves are too short, the energy becomes ultraviolet and beyond—X rays and gamma rays—and again, we can't see it. That's why scientists must build special telescopes for their sky studies. A star radiating exclusively in X-ray wavelengths would be completely invisible to us.

Light occupies a very small part of the electromagnetic spectrum, but it manages to radiate in many, many wavelengths. The size of these wavelengths determines what we call color. Light's longest wavelength is red, measuring a mere 7½ millionths of a meter. (A meter is about 39 inches, a little over a yard.) As the wavelengths get shorter and shorter, we start to see all the other colors in the spectrum: orange, yellow, green, blue, and finally violet.* Light packs a lot in a small space. The wavelength of violet is just 3 millionths of a meter shorter than red. Indeed, the human eye is very finely tuned.

When light Doppler shifts, it's because something causes the wavelengths to become either longer or shorter, but that's not such an easy trick to pull off. A train chugging along at 90 or even 40 miles an hour is plenty fast enough to create a Doppler shift with sound waves. But light's a much tougher customer. Forty miles an hour won't budge it. In fact, 40,000 miles an hour is too slow. For the Doppler shift to work on light, we almost have to "catch up" to the light. We have to

---

*It's time for you to meet Roy G. Biv, the color spectrum man. In order of their appearance in the spectrum we have: red, orange, yellow (ROY), green (G.), blue, indigo, violet (BIV). Indigo is a bluish purple and was probably included only so people could pronounce Roy's last name.

hit at least 20 percent light speed—about 40,000 miles a *second*.

It is the first week of your voyage, and already the solar system is far behind. "Wow!" you breathe, your eyes wide, just inches from the ship's massive viewing windows. The universe is ablaze with stars. They are all the stars that Earth's filtering atmosphere, its steadily increasing pollution and city lights, had erased.

Up here, in the icy-clear blackness that is everspace, the sky show plays to a delighted audience. Only a real expert— maybe you—will still be able to pick out Orion, and Pegasus, and Ursa Major from among the thick star glitter.

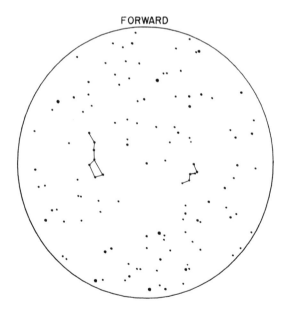

FORWARD

The view from a forward window before launch. All the stars are in the "right" places, and you can easily pick out the Big Dipper and the W-shape of Cassiopeia.

"Wow!" you say again because the universe has never looked so deep.

But this is only the beginning. . . .

Thirty percent light speed, and the passengers have settled into a familiar routine. Like worker ants, they come and go, hurrying down the corridors to their stations—day shift, swing shift, graveyard shift. Life aboard the *Albert Einstein* has become predictable. But outside, things are getting weird.

Is it your imagination, you wonder, or are there a lot more stars out there? You lean closer to the Great Window, squinting at the strange crowding of stars just ahead of the ship. New stars seem to be appearing as if by magic, drifting into

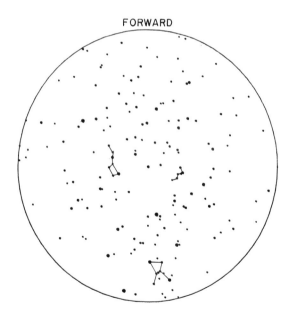

The Big Dipper and Cassiopeia begin to crush at 40 percent light speed, and Orion enters the field.

view from some far-off place beyond the edges of the window. Week after week you watch the stars, spilling over the rim of the window, pushing the old stars tighter and tighter together.

Where are they all coming from? you wonder, and then suddenly you know! You know why there are so many stars in front of the ship!

Excited, you run to catch up with one of the ship's little rim carts. As you climb aboard, the monitor lights up.

DESTINATION PLEASE

AFT, you decide, DELTA LEVEL, and gently press the keys. A slight lurch and you are moving, back, back, back to the rear of the ship and the very last window in the whole universe.

The ship is just over 40 percent light speed, but already the star field yawns like an open mouth, dark and cavernous. Slowly, steadily, the stars are migrating outward toward the edges of the aft window, leaving an expanding hole of space-black in the center. *This is where the stars in the front of the ship are coming from!*

A wave of dizziness washes over you: c-sickness someone once called it. It's so empty out there, as if the universe is folding in on itself, swallowing its own stars. Once upon a time the scientists thought there would be a glittering star-bow waiting to embrace the ship as it climbed toward light speed. But computer models in the 1980s showed something else, something far less romantic, but far more ghostly.

Sixty percent light speed and the phantom star drift continues, but now there is something else.

"Hey! Isn't that Aldebaran out there?" someone says.

You look and look again. Yes. Aldebaran, the fiery eye-

BACKWARD

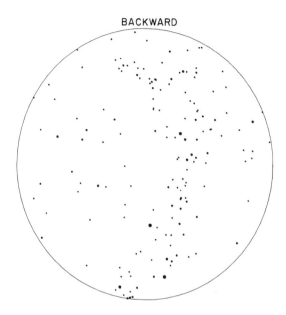

The view from the aft window is a little shocking! Where are the stars? Aberration is making them appear to drift around to the other side of the ship. Orion has already slipped away.

star of Taurus the bull. Big, red—crimson red, it used to be— but now Aldebaran looks brighter, more orangy yellow.

What's going on?

Hurriedly, you search for something familiar. Orion—your favorite constellation. The shoulders, the knees, the glittering belt . . . There! Over there! But, wait. That can't be Orion. Maybe that's his shape, but the star in his shoulder certainly doesn't look like Betelgeuse. Betelgeuse is a monstrous red giant. Like Aldebaran, this impostor is also orangy yellow. And Rigel at Orion's left knee!* What's happened to it? Ri-

---

*Since Orion is presumably facing us, Rigel would mark his left knee, although the star is on the right side of the constellation.

gel's supposed to be hot steel white. This Rigel is dull and sickly-looking.

Will somebody please tell me what in the name of Christian Doppler is going on here?

The shift has begun. As the *Albert Einstein* races on through the universe, light from the stars in front of the ship has less and less distance to travel to reach your eyes. So like the sound waves coming from an approaching train whistle, the light waves start to bunch up. This shortens their wavelengths, shifting the light toward the blue end of the spectrum. Stars that looked red when you were standing still back on Earth radiate now in orange, then yellow, and, after a while, white light. Dull, ruddy stars, like Betelgeuse, burst into brightness. Blue-white stars, which were already radiating at the short end, are pushed into the ultraviolet, where they dim and finally disappear.

Meanwhile, the stars in back of the ship are receding, moving farther and farther away. This puts them at ever increasing distances, and their light waves become stretched out. These longer waves kick the starlight up the electromagnetic spectrum toward the red end. So all the star colors behind you shift the other way. Red stars grow darker as their light waves stretch out to become infrared. Hot white stars lose their brilliance, while stars that radiated in the ultraviolet suddenly pop into view. At Einstein's magic speeds, the universe ripples and changes in a strange and wonderful dance of color.

But without question, the most startling effect of near-light-speed travel is the eerie, soundless gathering of the stars. The phenomenon is known as *aberration,* from an old Latin word meaning "to go astray." As the ship accelerates, the stars seem determined to keep up, to always stay ahead of the metallic intruder from planet Earth. All the stars in all

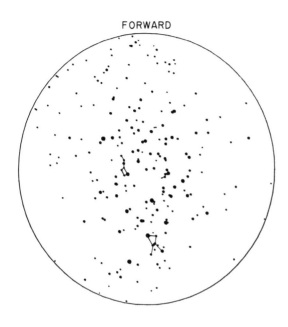

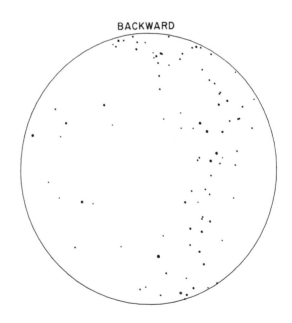

At 70 percent light speed, the Big Dipper and Cassiopeia are really crushed, while Orion has climbed higher into our field of view. Aft of the ship, though, the stars are nearly gone.

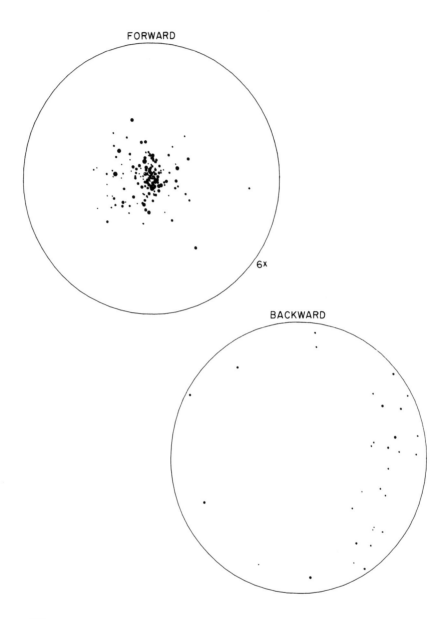

FORWARD

6ˣ

BACKWARD

*T*he universe at the edge of c, 99.98 percent light speed. All the stars have gathered tightly together. The familiar constellations are gone, and the universe itself has taken on a dull, ruddy glow. Aft of the ship, all is darkness and silence.

FIGURES CALCULATED AND COMPUTER-DRAWN BY JOHN MCKINLEY AND PAUL DOHERTY, OAKLAND UNIVERSITY, ROCHESTER, MICHIGAN the universe rush to a single point directly in front of the ship. Everywhere else there is deep, empty blackness, a still and silent dark. The ship moves on toward the solitary light that is no stars and all stars, that is every galaxy but no galaxy. And the faster the ship goes, the more concentrated the light source becomes.

A breath away from 186,282 miles per second and nearly a year into the voyage, the *Albert Einstein* seems desperately alone in the universe. The Milky Way and Andromeda, the galaxies known only by numbers, are all concentrated into a small, intense point of light dead ahead of the ship. The Doppler shift is now at its outermost limits, and even the cooling background temperature of the universe itself has taken on a dull glow.

Relativity has shrunk the ship and stretched out time. It has snatched the Earth from your grasp forever and ever, but it has given you the chance to ride the space waves to another galaxy. You have crossed time and space never to return.

The Magellanic clouds draw you to them. The great nebula in Andromeda is close enough to touch. The deeply mysterious quasars prepare to reveal their innermost secrets. You are a billion years from Earth because of Einstein's magic.

Someday, for real.

Will it be worth the ride? ★

CHAPTER 9

★

Faster than a
Speeding Photon

We will now take questions from the audience.

"Why can't anything go faster than light?"

Whoever said that?

"Oh, come on, Einstein said that. In the last chapter."

No, he didn't.

"He did so! 'Nothing can travel faster than light.' "

I believe what you read was, nothing can accelerate past the speed of light.

"Same thing."

Not quite. Let's think of light speed as a brick wall. Relativity says that rocket ships can't crash through the wall, but there's nothing in the equations about traveling on the other side of the wall.

"What!"

You look shocked. Listen, scientists tell us that there are

three categories of particles. First there are the tardyons, which always travel slower than light. A proton is a tardyon. The second class of particles is called luxons. *Lux* is Latin for "light," so a luxon travels at light speed precisely. Photons are luxons. And last but not least are the tachyons,* but they don't exist. At least, not so far.

Tachyons are from the land on the other side of the brick wall. They must travel faster than light. Remember how it required an infinite amount of energy to push our starship up to light speed? Well, a tachyon requires an infinite amount of energy to slow it down to light speed! As the tachyon loses energy, it speeds up. Makes you start to think about some kind of tachyon space drive, doesn't it?

"Not me," you say. "Tachyons don't exist."

But they could. In fact, there's a large loophole in quantum physics through which tachyons might be able to slip. It's called the "totalitarian principle." Pull up a chair. I'll tell you about it.

The physics lab was not always the bustling, exciting place it is today. Once upon a time, life among the slide rules and cloud chambers was slow and lazy. By 1932 the universe had been pretty much summed up in three kinds of particles—protons, neutrons, and wildly spinning electrons. A miniature solar system, they called it, and smiled contentedly. But it wasn't long before this elementary particle calm was shattered, first by the discovery of Dr. Dirac's positron and then by a veritable flood of strange and mysterious particles.

In the beginning, the particles appeared slowly, emerging one at a time from complicated equations. Some traveled at light speed and carried enough energy to bore their way

---

*Pronounced: **TACK** EE ONS

---

through planets. Others had lifetimes that lasted only microseconds before they burst apart in a shower of still more particles. To the physicists, it all must have seemed like some wild, free-for-all particle party.

There was, however, the little problem of proof. Most of the newcomers had never been seen. They were just "paper particles," brought to life only through fancy equations. Were there actually such things as leptons and quarks, or was it all just a bunch of math fuzz?

Fortunately, the physicists had a plan. Early on they had discovered that by smashing particles with supercharged bullets they could get the target particles to change into something else. Instead of breaking into fragments of itself, the original particle does a kind of magic act and turns into two, three, even four completely new particles. Sometimes the second-generation particle decays* and produces another set of particles. This continues until the collisions leave stable particles, particles that are perfectly content to stay just the way they are.

But the proof was in the demolition, so the physicists got out their blasters and shot away. However, forcing elementary particles to collide in a huge machine like a particle accelerator is far from easy. The speedway is miles long, the particles are virtually invisible, and they must be accelerated to speeds extremely close to light. So the physicists did not get results overnight. But eventually they managed to produce many of the oddball particles predicted by the equations.

Now, everything would have been just fine if only those darn tachyons hadn't shown up. All the other particles were

---

*This doesn't mean that the particle rots. Physicists use the word *decays* to describe a particle that keeps breaking down into other particles.

either tardyons or luxons, and they traveled at nice, rational speeds. The physicists could close their eyes and actually envision the particles. Even if they had slightly off-the-wall names like X Higgs bosons and antileptoquarks, the particles at least made sense and followed the rules of logic. They sped through the universe and didn't break anything.

But then there were the tachyons.

Get a load of this, said the equations: Particles that can never stand still. Particles that go faster and faster on less and less energy. Particles that, when they have no energy left at all, somehow manage to achieve infinite speed!

"Not possible!" shouted the physicists.

"Well, now, not so fast," replied Caltech physicist Murray Gell-Mann. "In a quantum collision, anything that isn't forbidden is compulsory," which is to say, unless there's a specific law against it, it's not only allowed to happen, it's required! All you need is an unlimited number of particle collisions and sooner or later, you'll wind up with just about everything—including tachyons! This "anything goes" policy is known as the totalitarian principle. So maybe relativity forbids us from stepping over the light barrier, but it's perfectly okay to start off on the other side of the barrier. And so, impossible as it sounds, tachyons are allowed in the strange world of quantum physics.

Wow! Find the tachyons! Build a tachyon-powered starship!

It is tempting, isn't it? But as you shall see, this faster-than-light answer to our space travel dreams is one of the biggest nightmares in all of science.

Those of you who were here for Chapter 8 know that very high speeds have a rather nasty effect on time. As a spaceship draws closer and closer to The Great Einstein Barrier, time gets slower, and s-l-o-w-e-r, and s—l—o—w—e—r. But if time stands still at light speed exactly, what happens on the other side of light speed?

Welcome to the nightmare. On the other side of light speed where tachyons run and play, time flows *backward*. A journey in a tachyon-powered ship would take you—not faster—but back into the past. If you headed for the Whirlpool galaxy, 37 million light-years away, you would return home before you left, making for a curious situation indeed.

"Hey, look, you guys!" you'd say, waving a pack of freshly developed snapshots. "Pictures from the Whirlpool."

The beautiful Whirlpool galaxy lies over 37 million light-years away.

HALE OBSERVATORIES

"Aw, who are you trying to kid?" little Iggy Cappilardi would say. "You're not going to the Whirlpool galaxy until the end of the month."

"No, no. I went, and now I'm back. I left on March thirtieth and today's . . . let's see . . ."

"February eleventh."

Well, this is certainly creepy. In six weeks, you're supposed to leave for a trip that you've already taken. So did you go or didn't you go?

But you must have gone! You have memories of the ship, the other passengers, the places you visited.

Yes, but if you really went and came back, your friends should all be dead by now. Almost 75 million years would have passed on Earth. Nuts! you think. Maybe the Earth shouldn't even be here!

You wonder what will happen during the next six weeks. Will some mysterious force drive you in a zombie sort of way to repeat every single thing you did before you went to the Whirlpool galaxy, allegedly for the first time? Will your life be like the rerun of a movie?

All at once, a terrible, hair-raising possibility occurs to you. What if your journey into the past has trapped you in a time loop? Over and over, for all eternity you will travel to the Whirlpool galaxy and return. Again and again you will board the ship on March 30 and come home on February 11. You will meet your friends in Quark Park and have the same conversation, three times, four times, a hundred thousand times, billions and billions of times.

Nervously, you glance at your friends who are in a very heated discussion about your photographs from the Whirlpool, and you distinctly hear the word *bogus* being thrown around. But the pictures aren't bogus. You took them with the very camera your friends gave you as a going-away present.

Only they haven't given it to you yet.

But they must have because it's right there in your knapsack. At least you think it's in your knapsack.

Go ahead. Take a look, you tell yourself. You swallow hard. *That's okay. Maybe later,* because now you've just thought of another problem.

Suppose you refuse to get on the ship bound for the Whirlpool galaxy. Suppose you deliberately leave your house too late to catch the connecting shuttle. Then what? By changing the past you will have changed the future, so if you don't go to the Whirlpool galaxy this time, how could you have possibly gone the first time? No. Wait. That's not right. Your return from the Whirlpool is in the future even though you put it back into the past, so by changing the future you will have changed the past. Wow! What a mess!

As you walk home, you begin to understand why fiddling with the past is serious business. You wonder why it looks so easy when they do it in the movies. The main character just jumps into a machine, shoots back into the past, adjusts a couple of things that went wrong, and everybody lives happily ever after. But in real life it's a lot more complicated.

You round the corner of Baryon Street and spot your house at the far end of the block, the one with the green shutters and the lopsided fence gate. Oops. No. Your dad fixed that gate about a week before you left for the Whirlpool. But as you approach the house you can see that the gate is still swinging drunkenly on its hinges.

"Hey . . . who broke the gate?" you squawk.

But then you remember. It's only February 11. Your father will not repair the gate for another five weeks. Jeez! This is creepy!

You take the back porch steps two at a time and push open the door. "Ma! I'm home!"

But the voice you hear in reply isn't your mother's.

"Who's there?" it demands.

You step cautiously into the living room and your blood freezes. Standing before you at the head of the stairs is a frighteningly familiar face. The face has your nose. It has your hair. It has your ears and your eyes.

"Who are you?" you screech, but, of course, you already know.

"What do you mean, 'Who am I?' " the you-who-isn't-you replies. "Who are you?"

And then, the bizarre reality of it all sinks in. Your journey into the past has rather inconveniently brought you face to face with yourself. Here is the You Number 1 who has not yet left for the Whirlpool galaxy, while you are the You Number 2 who has gone on the trip and returned.

"Oh, no!" you both moan. "Mom's gonna go nuts when she sees this!"

Certainly an understatement, and the dual yous are not very popular with the physicists either. They are hard pressed, they say, to imagine two people who are one and the same. It goes against all reason and contradicts many of the things we have come to accept about the world. Things like, "A person can't be in two places at once," or "Two things can't occupy the same space."

Physicists object to multiple yous, not because of a mathematical equation that doesn't work, but because it poses a big logic problem. No matter how we twist the physics, there can only be one original bona fide you. Identical twins and clones may look like each other, but they are separate and distinct individuals, not the same person twice. But by traveling into the past, you have caused another you to pop into existence, the same you you are now, only at an earlier time. It's as though an old photograph had suddenly come to life. And the more trips into the past you take, the more yous you create!

"Okay, okay," you might say. "No trips into the near past, the 'me' past. Then why don't you impose travel restrictions? You know, blackout periods, like the airlines have."

All right. Let's try it.

The bespectacled ticket agent leans over the wooden counter. "Birth date?"

"March 4, 2054," you reply.

A rustling of schedules. "All right. That's your cutoff point. No trips beyond that. No . . . wait a minute. Gotta add the nine months, I suppose, while your mom was pregnant with you. That brings us back into 2053. Here we go. No trips beyond August 2053."

"August what? Which day? August 4?"

Eyes bulge behind a pair of white rhinestone frames. "I don't know August what. How long was your mom pregnant with you? How many days exactly?"

"How am I supposed to know that? Look, lady, I didn't want to go that close back anyway. I want to see the dinosaurs. Can't you just give me a ticket for 65 million years ago? Any day is fine."

A long, hard glare. "No, I cannot. Rules are rules."

This is entirely too much fine-tuning for the physicists to be comfortable with. If time travel is possible, it will ultimately have to be spelled out in a series of mathematical equations, just as time dilation is explained by relativity equations. But when there are a lot of exceptions and special conditions, the equations become long and complicated, and physicists usually have to use "fudge factors." A fudge factor is a number that is inserted so the equations can be solved. Physicists don't like fudge factors because experience has shown them that the best model is usually the simplest. So this time-travel-with-extenuating-circumstances idea is feeble at best.

But if you're not yet convinced that time travel is pure Buck Rogers, here is perhaps the worst-case scenario of all. It is a tachyon trip that brings you right back to your hometown before you were conceived. Who, then, are you?

"Mama!" Your arms open wide as you approach the young girl bent over a freshly seeded flower bed.

Her head turns. She is perhaps sixteen, seventeen, tops.

You kneel down beside her. "Mama!" and plant a kiss on her cheek.

"*What!*" she screams and jumps to her feet, horrified at the very idea of being anybody's mother, especially with cheerleading tryouts coming up next week. "Who are you, anyway?"

And you, of course, are at a complete loss to explain yourself.

Shocked and hurt by your mother's behavior, you flee to the streets and take up with a gang of toughs who decide to kidnap your mother and hold her hostage until she is too old to have children.

But this scheme doesn't sit well with you one bit. "Then how am I supposed to get born?" you want to know.

The top tough shrugs his shoulders. "Beats me," he replies. "Maybe you won't get born at all. Maybe you'll just vanish."

If all this is starting to sound like a Saturday morning cartoon, it's because the physics is breaking down. Cause and effect are no longer operating. We have an effect (your obvious presence) without a cause (your birth), and this cannot be. No matter how bizarre events may become because of the effects of relativity, the world must still operate by cause and effect.

But in a last-ditch effort to save at least the logistics of time travel, some scientists have proposed what might be called an alternate reality program. In the alternate reality program, you can go back and forth through time as much as you like, changing the past, fiddling with other people's lives, and things will still be all right. Why? Because there is no one "correct" reality.

Perhaps, say the scientists, there are an infinite number of scenarios. Even if the gang of toughs dreams up twenty different ways to prevent your mother from giving birth to you, there will always be an alternate future that provides for your birth. In what is a kind of combination predestination/free choice universe, every possible past and future has already been established, but the choice is left up to you. This way of looking at things doesn't break any of the rules of physics, but it does make reality something of a free-for-all.

The exact opposite is a reality in which the future is a total blank, developing only when you get there. You have one shot, and whatever choices you make are forever unchangeable. Of course, this means that you can travel neither forward into the future—since there isn't any future yet—nor backward into the past because if you did, you wouldn't exist.

Despite its apparent impossibility, though, time travel continues to hold our imagination captive. Who hasn't dreamed of spinning the dial and returning to third grade so we can give big, fat Bugsy McSkuggs the left hook he deserves? Or slip back just for a minute to hand in the missing book report that spelled ruin in seventh grade? Who hasn't wanted to floor the accelerator on the time machine and step out, an eye blink later, into the still air on the mountain where Jesus delivered his sermon? Or into the room with the windows flung wide where Galileo first turned his small telescope to the heavens? Or to a steamy, Mesozoic swamp populated by the massive animals we would one day call terrible lizards?

And who hasn't wanted to go back, all the way back, just to see how the whole thing began?

Driven by tachyons, our ship, the *Cronos I*, could carry us 4.5 billion years into the past to witness the birth of our solar system. Astronomers have drawn a picture for us based on their best theories about how stars and planets form, but the *Cronos I* could actually show us. We would see the great swirling nebula slowly condense into a pale protosun and then suddenly ignite as gravity lit its fusion fires. We would watch the outer cloud layers break up into small, tumbling bodies—nameless protoplanets at first, and then Mercury and Venus, Earth and Mars, and all the others. We could be there to see Mars capture its two little moons and Saturn earn its golden rings. We would at last find out why Uranus is so tilted on its axis, where the asteroids came from, what went wrong on Venus to transform it into a sulphuric-acid nightmare.

Then the biologists on board would take the helm and steer the *Cronos I* ahead to a cooling Earth just before life began to stir in the oceans. Armed with video cameras, they would watch and wait as a bunch of lightning-charged chemicals became the miracle that is us. Or perhaps they would see something else.

A few astronomers have suggested that Earth may have been "seeded" by an advanced civilization from another galaxy. It is too much of a long shot, they say, for life to have sprung up spontaneously. So maybe we were carried here in ships or sent in small, sealed capsules and our amino acids released into the cloud tops to fall as rain upon the land. Maybe we have been looking in the wrong place for the aliens. Maybe the aliens are us.

But the ultimate time trip would belong to the particle physicists who would assume command of the *Cronos I* after the biologists. The physicists would set the final course that would plunge the ship backward into the nothing nowhere moment of the big bang. Poised upon an impossible observation deck, everyone on board would watch the creation of time and space. In an instant, in the time it takes to breathe, all secrets would be revealed, all questions answered.

If we could travel faster than light . . .

Well, now. That would make quite a movie, wouldn't it? So our first order of business is to find the tachyons. What are our chances? Even though relativity theory allows tachyons, that's no guarantee they actually exist. Maybe they're just a distant memory of what once was. Like so many other strange particles, tachyons might have been created when—and only when—the universe burst into existence. But since tachyons can't stand still, off they went. The only problem is where they could have gone.

In those first few microseconds after the big bang, space had just barely begun to expand, so it would have been pretty hard to get lost; hard, at least, if you were a normal, forward moving particle. But tachyons move backward in time, so some scientists have suggested that these little jokers returned to the point of the big bang. And then what?

Obviously, say the scientists, the tachyons must have entered either an earlier universe—the one that came before ours—or some kind of alternate universe. That means tachyons are, and will forever be, unreachable. If we can't climb over the light-speed fence and the tachyons can't crawl under it, there's not much hope of us ever getting together.

But maybe Dr. Gell-Mann is right after all. Maybe with enough particle smashups, we'll eventually produce some tachyons.

Still, tachyons are such oddball particles, it's hard to imagine ever being able to use them as a space-time drive. For openers, we'd need two separate engines—a conventional one to get the spaceship up to light speed, and some kind of tachyon system for the time travel part of the trip. Right now, rocket engineers are struggling to turn the Bussard ramjet into reality. Mention tachyons to them and they'd probably throw their blueprints at you.

We also have the problem of the time gap, the moment when the ship reaches light speed exactly and time stands still. What happens to all the passengers? Held suspended by relativity, they cannot move. Their hearts pause in mid-beat. They have become prisoners of time, as still and lifeless as the pictures they brought from home.

But worse, far worse, is the fact that the would-be time travel passengers will remain suspended forever. There can be no autopilot, no faithful, unfailing computer that automatically shifts into tachyon drive because *the ship is also a victim of time dilation.* It too has been stopped. So even if we did come up with a tachyon drive, we couldn't use it.

And finally, there are the relativity effects of faster-than-light travel. If the passengers age more slowly as the ship approaches light speed and stop aging completely at light speed, it is logical to assume that beyond light speed, everybody in the ship starts getting younger. But even more bizarre, as the time ship accelerates, the passengers are carried farther and farther into their own past until they simply pop out of existence.

The oldest person aboard, Violet LaVie, has managed to hang on, although just barely. She is five, or at least she will be in April. Violet is the only one who can bring the ship to its final destination, some lonely outpost in the Yukon in the late 1800s. Violet is certainly smart enough to tell the ship's computer what to do, but her instructions can never be carried out.

Before the ship can arrive, it has to slow down. But as it slows down, the flow of backward time gradually begins to reverse itself until it jumps the light-speed wall and is flowing normally again. So there is no way the time ship can ever "land." It may reach the goal timewise, but it can't get there spacewise.

If the scientists do indeed find tachyons one day, they will have solid proof that something in our universe can travel faster than light. Unfortunately, that something will not be us. But perhaps it's just as well. Any decent universe has rules, and without these rules, it just wouldn't be as much fun to live here. There'd be nothing to break. ★

CHAPTER 10

★

Into the Tunnel

*H*a, ha, ha!" screamed the evil Zorg Zorgenstein. "Now I've got you, you miserable Earthlings!"

The captain of the *Betty Lou and Harold* stuck out his tongue at the little voice from the interstellar radio. "Oh yeah?" he growled. "Just watch."

He pressed the ship's intercom. "Hey, Loretta, how far are we from the tunnel?"

A crackle of static. "Chief, please don't call it a tunnel. This isn't Earth."

The captain made a face. "Yeah, yeah, yeah. Black hole. It's a black hole. So how far?"

"Four-point-oh-six light-minutes," the navigator replied.

"*Heh, heh, heh!*" It was Zorgenstein again.

"Oh, shut up!" snarled the captain.

"He can't hear you," said Loretta. "The communicator's broken."

"Figures! First we run out of spaghetti sauce and now the communicator's on the blink. What about the plunger? Is that busted too?"

"Chief, please don't call it a plunger. It sounds like we have a stuffed-up toilet."

"Whatever it is, then," said the captain. "Will we be able to make the jump when we get to the tun—I mean, the black hole?"

"That's affirmative."

"Good!" the captain replied. "Get us outta here. That wise guy alien is starting to bug me."

And in the grand and sweeping tradition of the cheap science fiction novel, the captain and crew of the *Betty Lou and Harold* plunged into the throat of the black hole and escaped. The end.

But for science—the real kind—it may be just the beginning.

Everybody assumes that Einstein invented black holes, but it was actually the eighteenth-century French mathematician and astronomer Pierre Simon Laplace who thought of them first. Laplace suggested that there might be stars whose gravity was so powerful, nothing—not even light—could escape their surface.* The unfortunate star would then wink out and live the rest of its days in total darkness. But this somewhat radical idea didn't sit too well with the stuffed shirts in Laplace's day, so black holes were jammed back into the astronomy closet to await the twentieth century.

---

*Gravity determines how fast a spaceship must be moving if it intends to escape an object's clutches. This is, of course, escape velocity, made famous in Chapter 1.

When Einstein revived the concept of the black hole, he helped himself by putting his math where his mouth was. His theory of general relativity showed, in no uncertain terms, that such things really could exist. Black holes, said Einstein, are formed when large, dense stars reach the end of their life spans and blow apart in a violent explosion. Most of the star's material is thrown off to expand outward as a spreading gas cloud, while the remaining core collapses in on itself. The staggering power of gravity deals the final blow, crushing the star's burned-out core into an infinitely small point. The result of this rather unseemly death is a black hole.

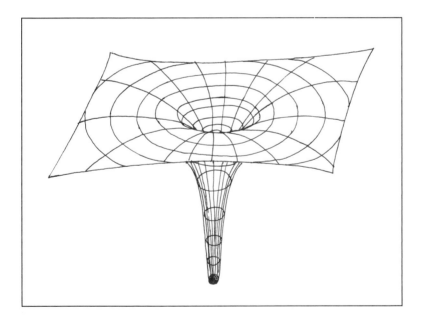

The creation of a black hole. A black hole is so dense, it distorts space in a bizarre way. The black hole's gravitational field is powerful enough to prevent light from escaping up the "funnel."

Since black holes don't emit light, they're impossible to detect with optical telescopes, but there are other ways of catching them. For instance, black holes do not sit idly by minding their own business. They can't. Their gravity is much too intense and has disastrous effects on everything in the neighborhood. Careless stars that stray too close are gobbled down whole, while those a little farther away are held captive like flies in a spider web. As the prisoner star orbits the black hole, it slowly loses material to the black hole's deep gravity well. The star's gas is sucked down into the black hole, similar to the way crumbs and other debris are pulled toward a vacuum cleaner nozzle. The gas spirals around the perimeter, forming a glowing ring called an accretion disk, before it vanishes forever into the black hole's hungry jaws.

This slow death by gravity would be something to see, all right: a stretched-out, badly distorted star with curling tendrils of gas disappearing into a zero point of nothingness. It would also be rather telling proof of a black hole on the loose. But unfortunately, the closest suspect is over six thousand light-years away. While a telescope will easily pick up the victimized star, it won't show us any detail. The target appears as a tiny point of light and nothing more. However, this doesn't necessarily mean the black hole gets away from us.

As gas from the black hole's companion star plunges to oblivion, it is heated to tremendous temperatures. This causes extremely intense X rays to burst from the outer rim of the black hole. Now, there's nothing especially weird about X rays emanating from a point in space. But if the radiation appears to be coming out of nowhere, then astronomers start to think black hole.

Another clue that can indicate the presence of a black hole

is the stellar two-step. Imagine, if you will, a star chugging along through space. We'll call him Fred. Thanks to Newton's first law of motion, Fred's path is pretty much a straight line. "A moving object," Newton might have said if he were around today, "keeps moving in a straight line unless something comes along and gives it a shove." So Fred makes his way across the background of stars along a route that is boring and predictable.

But now let's give Fred a dancing partner. Call her Ginger. If Fred and Ginger can get close enough, their mutual gravitation will lock them in an orbital embrace, and they will become a binary system. Off they will go, through the night and the music, turning circles around each other. However, by partnering up, Fred loses his ability to move in a straight line.* He may want to go straight, but at the same time he is forced to keep orbiting Ginger. So if Fred the star had chalk dust on his shoes, you would see that his path is actually a spiral, like a strand of naturally curly hair.

Astronomers who search for extrasolar planets look for the spirals in a star's path, but it takes patience and a lot of fine measurements. The gravitational effects of a small planet on what is certain to be a much larger star are extemely hard to detect. But suppose the star's companion is really *big*. Instead of being lightweight and delicate like Ginger, the companion is more like some guy named Bruno, many, many more times massive than Fred. What happens to poor Fred? You can probably imagine it. Fred gets yanked and yanked but good. Bruno's gravity flings Fred around and around and creates— not nice little curly spirals—but big glitches in Fred's path across the sky.

---

*The same thing happens to Ginger.

Quickly, we aim a telescope in the direction of Fred the star. Sure enough, there he is, but no matter how carefully we scan the area, we can't find anything even remotely resembling a massive companion star. And so, we are left to draw one of two conclusions: Either the invisible companion is too dim to be seen in the blinding stellar glare, or Fred's companion is a black hole.

As it happens, several years ago X-ray astronomers noticed this same glitchy two-step in a star located in the northern hemisphere constellation Cygnus the swan. The star in question was the brilliant supergiant HDE 226868, which, by the way, also happened to be sending out huge bursts of X rays. This promptly gave the astronomers goose bumps. "Whoa!" they said. "That's way too much radiation for a star like HDE 226868," and they decided that something very fishy was going on out there.

Eventually, the astronomers managed to come up with a shocking set of measurements. HDE 226868, they announced, is apparently rotating around an as-yet-unseen object at the breathless pace of 5 days, 14 hours, and 24 minutes! (As a comparison, it takes the Earth, which is just a fraction of the size of HDE 226868, 365 days to make one orbit around the sun. Clearly, HDE 226868 is really motoring!) Speeds like that catch astronomers' attentions, and immediately, an all-out search was launched to find the phantom object.*

The months passed. Nothing.

Suggestions were offered. A brown dwarf, maybe. Brown dwarfs are still only theory. Some astronomers believe them

---

*Astronomers are able to "erase" the bright glare around a star so they can search for smaller, less luminous stars in the neighborhood. Very often, one big shot in a multiple system will completely drown out its companions. Astronomers first used this "artificial eclipse" on telescopic images of the sun so they could track Mercury, which is easily lost in the sun's glare.

to be a kind of semistar, semiplanet; an object that never quite ignited but remains in a stage of stellar twilight. But a brown dwarf would not have the mass needed to hold HDE 226868 in orbit. And for pretty much the same reason, HDE 226868's companion couldn't be a planet either.

The think tank bubbled and churned until the scientists had eliminated virtually everything—pulsars, neutron stars, and all the other objects in the astronomy arsenal. Except one.

A black hole.

Without fanfare, the astronomers christened the object Cygnus X-1. The X means it's an intense X-ray source.

Since then, astronomers have unearthed quite a number of black hole candidates, the most promising of which is LMC X-3. LMC X-3 is a violent X-ray producer in the Large Magellanic Cloud, one of two companion galaxies visible from the southern hemisphere. LMC X-3 is not close. It lies some 160,000 light-years away, which makes studying it quite a challenge. Still, the three astronomers in hot pursuit of this black hole are almost certain they have spotted LMC X-3's companion. It is a large, luminous star whose orbital period around LMC X-3 is a shocking 1 day, 3 hours, 24 minutes, and a handful of seconds. Based on this, the astronomers have been able to calculate LMC X-3's mass. Incredibly, even though they can't—and probably never will—see this object, they're almost positive it's a black hole. Anything that massive and invisible just has to be.

Black holes have certainly come of age, capturing the fancy of even the most conservative physicists, and it's no wonder. Everybody likes a good mystery. Here is an object that is not really an object. It is a place, but time and space are so warped there, it seems more like an unplace, or maybe an antiplace.

But its weirdness doesn't prevent it from having three distinct and genuine geographical features. In order of entry they are:

The *Schwarzschild radius,* named after Karl Schwarzschild, who first described it. The Schwarzschild radius is the dying star's point of no return. As the star's core begins to collapse, its radius gets smaller and smaller and smaller. If the star is able to squeeze its core down to a certain critical size—the Schwarzschild radius—it becomes a black hole. If not, it ends its life as a slowly cooling ball of stellar ash.

The Schwarzschild radius is different for every star. That's because it's proportional to the star's original mass. (This is similar to the method used by veterinarians to figure out how much medicine to give your sick puppy. The dosage is based on your dog's weight.) A star about the same size as our sun has a Schwarzschild radius of just under two miles. For a star built more along the lines of the Earth, the Schwarzschild radius is less than half an inch!*

The Schwarzschild radius is the first checkpoint. Once the star hits this dimension, there's no turning back. The star has now become so dense, its escape velocity exceeds light speed, and the star winks out. Gravity forces the star to continue collapsing, leaving behind a kind of ghostly borderline called the *event horizon.*

The event horizon is the door to death through which nothing ever returns. What goes in, stays in. Period. If by some terrible miscalculation you should find yourself crossing the event horizon, you will be sucked down, down, down into the deep gravity well that surrounds the black hole, although you're not likely to see much along the way. The instant you fall in, you will be stretched out like a wad of

---

*Less than the diameter of a dime

bubble gum. If your head is closer to the black hole's surface than your feet, it will feel the nasty effects of the gravity first. Then, in a matter of microseconds, your neck, your shoulders, your torso and arms, your legs, and finally your feet will be drawn toward the center of the black hole, turning you into the tallest, skinniest dead person in the universe. So future space pilots would be doing themselves a big favor by taking along a good set of maps when they leave home.

Once the black hole creates an event horizon, gravity forces it to crush down even further until it becomes a nothing, nowhere, nospace dot called a *singularity*. Even to a physicist, a singularity is weird. It is infinitely small, but at the same time, infinitely dense. So this thing that has no spacial dimensions at all somehow manages to weigh more than it's possible for anything to weigh—except maybe another singularity.

Everything that falls into the black hole becomes part of the singularity. There, all the accepted laws of physics completely break down, and no one knows what goes on. It is, most effectively, the very end of the known universe; total oblivion.

Scientists have suggested that the universe itself was created from a singularity. This, they say, may have developed when a previous universe, old and dying and enlarged to its fullest volume, contracted back in on itself. But since everything—including the entire space-time fabric—would have been drawn into the singularity, there wouldn't have been any place to put an event horizon. So all that remained was what scientists call a *naked singularity*. A naked singularity has no gates, no border guards, no DO NOT ENTER signs. It is a raw point, an "incision" in the universe where an impossible physics exists.

Many physicists feel that naked singularities cannot exist because they are protected by the so-called principle of cosmic censorship. This basically says that the heart of a black hole is entirely too strange for us to see. But even if naked singularities could exist, they wouldn't be any help at all to star pilots looking to short-hop it through a black hole. In fact, a singularity—naked or not—is a pilot's worst nightmare. Here's why:

You have probably noticed that as the water runs out of your bathtub, it swirls around the drain in a counterclockwise motion. This occurs because the Earth is rotating on its axis, carrying the water along with it. But what maybe you didn't know is that in the very center of the whirlpool there is a "hole," a dry spot, similar to the eye of a hurricane. So if you have a steady hand, you can slip a thin wooden shish kebab skewer into the middle of the swirling water without it getting wet.

Now, if you had a glass bathtub and glass pipes, you would see that the dry spot created by the swirling water tapers down and eventually pinches off, so at some point, the skewer will get wet. But black holes are not bathtub drains, and the "dry spot" in a black hole is more of a funnel shape. It may be narrow, but it never quite closes up, so the result is a little passageway, a tunnel, into the black hole. There are, however, a couple of tricky aspects to all of this.

For one thing, the tunnel doesn't lie in the center of the black hole. How can it? The singularity is in the center! Instead, the only safe way down is close to the inside wall. The second problem is the tunnel's width.

It stands to reason that the more massive the original star that becomes the black hole, the wider its passable tunnel. But the star had better be very, very massive. A star five times the sun's mass will have a passable tunnel less than 1,000 feet in diameter. Even if the star is ten times the sun's mass, it's still going to be a tight fit. This means a star captain will need nerves of steel, extremely precise coordinates, and a very skinny ship to stand even a half-baked chance. But let's assume our pilot is Adelaid "the Threader" Kushkowski and that, in Adelaid's words, "There ain't no black hole that can hold me." So in she goes, lock, stock, and interstellar rocket.

But just exactly where is she going? To find out, we'll have to call on Einstein.

For several decades now, scientists have been debating the shape of the universe. Before Einstein, everyone simply assumed that the universe looked like a big, round balloon. But then Einstein suggested the universe might have a more exotic shape. Maybe, he said, it looks like a saddle and folds over on itself. This would give the universe a "right" side and a "left" side (where the stirrups would hang) with a carved-out hollow area in between (the part that fits over the horse).

Now, in the olden days, the average star buckaroo could have cared less about the shape of the universe. Everyone figured there was only one way to cross the cosmos; the slow way, dragging along, one boring light-year at a time. Then in 1935, Einstein and his colleague Nathan Rosen found a shortcut, but in order for it to work, they needed a saddle-shaped universe.

Einstein and Rosen imagined a black hole dense enough to stretch the fabric of space until it ripped. This tear provided an entrance to the shortcut, but if the universe were a sphere, the opening wouldn't lead anywhere. It couldn't, since the universe was all there was and there was no such thing as another side. But if the universe were shaped like a saddle,* the hole would open—not into space—but into the cavity between the two sides of the saddle. It would have to be, concluded Einstein and Rosen, another universe! You may know Einstein's and Rosen's alternate universe as something called hyperspace.†

So here's the plot: The ultradense black hole tears the space fabric on one side of the universe, barrels its way across hyperspace, and punches through space on the other side

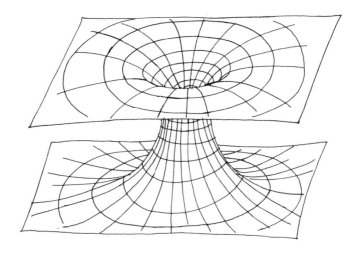

*A*n *Einstein/Rosen bridge. The shortcut to a distant part of the universe?*

---

*This image is extremely hard to picture. You are probably imagining a 100% gen-you-ine, DEE-LUX leather saddle floating in space, so your saddle does have another side. Einstein's saddle, however, isn't floating in anything. It *is* the universe.

†Science fiction author John Campbell was certainly Johnny-on-the-spot for this one. The minute Einstein and Rosen came up with the idea of a universe that lay outside our own, Campbell christened it hyperspace.

---

of the "saddle." *Voilà!* A tunnel has been created connecting two very distant parts of the universe.

This space-time tunnel, which became known as the Einstein/Rosen bridge, provides Threader Kushkowski with an instantaneous link, so she is across it in practically no time at all. But the fun's not over yet because she still has to contend with the rather perilous exit ramp. Threader may have entered via a black hole, but it's a cinch she can't use one to get out. Black holes, if you remember, never give up the goods once they have gobbled something down. So what Einstein and Rosen needed was the exact opposite of a black hole—a white hole!

White holes presumably have everything that black holes have except in reverse. But the best part—certainly for Threader and her crew—is the assumption that white holes spit matter out instead of swallowing it. A trip through a white hole would hardly be a sleigh ride, but technically, it's an exit, and hey! when you've gone that far, you're not likely to be too fussy.

But let's return to reality, here. Does the Einstein/Rosen bridge even have a prayer? After all, it's not as though Einstein and Rosen met one Sunday afternoon in Rosen's garage, slapped together a spaceship, and went for a spin through the nearest black hole. It's not as if they *tested* their idea. As a matter of fact, even the most basic aspects of this thing are a headache. For instance, there's the inconvenience of not ever knowing your destination. Since there are an infinite number of possible exit ramps, and since black holes don't divulge any information, you always enter wearing a navigational blindfold.

What's that? You think we ought to send out a team of cartographers to map the area on the other side of the bridge? Interesting idea, but how do we get everybody home when they're done? The only sure route is back across the bridge, but we can't go that way. Remember? WHITE HOLE! DO NOT ENTER! So unless the crew is willing to wander around until they spot a familiar star cluster or something, they're pretty much stuck out there. And if by some miracle they do make it home, will there even be a home? While time dilation is subtracting millennia from the explorers' lives, it is adding those same millennia to the Earth and all the people on it.

Another rather disturbing part of traveling across the Einstein/Rosen bridge is the nature of the terrain. While the black and white holes are both a part of our universe, the bridge might not be. Einstein and Rosen suggested that it might traverse an alternate universe, but they didn't have the vaguest idea what that universe might be like. It could be built according to a totally different set of physical laws where—who knows?—maybe time flows backward and tachyons run the show. It could even be a universe made entirely of antimatter—and that would not be so good at all. The second you stepped onto the bridge from the black hole, you'd encounter the antimatter and explode in a burst of pure energy.

But probably the biggest difficulty with the Einstein/Rosen bridge is the tremendous odds against it ever forming in the first place. The whole thing depends on a long shot; the black hole has to be standing still. This might not sound very important, but in space, movement is everything. Astronomers have yet to find a planet or a moon, a star or a galaxy, that isn't rotating. Some rotate clockwise, some counterclockwise; but they all turn slowly, moderately, quickly, or at daring breakneck speeds on their axes. Certainly the star will be rotating before it becomes a black hole, so why should it suddenly stop rotating just because it collapses? In fact, if anything, its rotation rate will likely speed up as gravity causes it to contract (the way ice skaters speed up their spins by pulling in their arms). So we are apparently stuck with a bunch of rotating black holes.

But, hey! Maybe that's just exactly what we want!

During the early 1960s, New Zealand mathematician Roy Kerr was working on rotating black hole equations. In physics, an equation is a suggestion, a mathematical model. It says that something might be able to exist, but to find out for sure, you have to solve the equation.

The black hole equations were killers. They were long and very complex, but if Kerr could get everything to balance, he would have a clear mathematical picture of a rotating black hole. So he pushed on through the scrap paper sea washing over his desk. And then one day in 1963 the solution revealed itself. This was it! Einstein's extraordinary stellar object had come to life again, only this time it was spinning. And this time it had a trapdoor.

Kerr's rotating black hole is a wild and woolly object. It is spinning furiously on its axis and distorting the fabric of space-time almost beyond description. But if you know the way in, it will carry you to times and places you never dreamed of. If you know the way in . . .

Like all black holes, a rotating black hole has a singularity, but it is not a bottomless, dimensionless point. It is, instead, a ring. This ring formation happens only because the black hole is spinning. If we could somehow force the black hole to apply the brakes, the singularity would become a point again.

The ring singularity provides us with a safe—although rather narrow—entrance into the black hole. The only requirements are that you must go in at an angle and match the speed and direction of the black hole's rotation. If you go in straight, you will be whipped out to the edges of the singularity, like cake batter in a rotating mixer. But by following the black hole's spin rate, you are, in a sense, camouflaging yourself. You're fooling the black hole into thinking you're part of the action.

But despite how amazingly easy travel through a rotating black hole sounds, don't go looking to book passage just yet. You must remember that we're not talking about the Chesapeake Bay Bridge-Tunnel here. Black holes, rotating or not (but especially rotating ones), are extremely strange objects, perched on the very brink of the known universe. A quick shoot through Kerr's rotating black hole leads to a region of what physicists call negative space-time, and this is not something you want to mess with.

Scientists have suggested that negative space-time would mean negative gravity, a back-flowing of time, inverted space (whatever that might be), and a whole host of unpleasantries. So technically, a spaceship could navigate a rotating black hole, but in light of this negative space-time stuff, you've got to ask yourself, what on Earth for?

Is this the end of high-speed chases? Will star captains always have to take the long way around to escape the bug-eyed aliens? Are the tunnels forever closed to our ships?

With a deep sigh, the physicists nod their heads. "Not advisable to jump into black holes," they say. "Not a smart thing. Take the back roads."

But the science fiction writers lie in wait.

"Psst! Over here!" they whisper. Their eyes are twinkling. "Hey, kid! Wanna know a shortcut?"

And of course, you do.

The dream never dies. ★

CHAPTER 11

★

The Quest for Zorg

org Zorgenstein sat in front of his intergalactic transaxial three-dimensional video-booster and roared with laughter.

"Now what?" asked his wife, sliding a crescent wrench into her tool caddy.

Zorg guffawed. "Football! It's a riot!"

"Are you watching Earth games again? Honestly, Zorg, I don't know why you just sit here, day after day, twiddling that locator dial and eating quaso chips. If you fixed the ship you could go to Earth and sit in the stadium like everyone else."

Zorg waved her off. "I'm fine, perfectly fine. I don't need to go schlepping across the universe and maybe catching a cold or something. I can see everything I want right from here. . . . Hey! What's that thing?"

Zorg's wife leaned toward the screen. "What thing?"

"That thing. See that guy in the flannel shirt? That thing on his head."

"It's a clapping hat."

"What does it do?"

"It claps. The two felt hands on the sides are attached to strings. When the man pulls the strings, the hands clap."

"Yeow!" screamed Zorg, leaping out of his seat and upsetting the bowl of quaso chips. "*I want one!*"

"Then you'll have to go to Earth," said his wife. "Sometimes there's just no substitute for space travel."

But traveling to the stars takes money. Big money. First we need a workable ship design, and since we are not even close to one yet, you can figure on several billion dollars just for the research alone. Then there's the cost of building the prototype. Do we put the whole thing together down here on Earth where we will be stuck with the problem of "fuel bulking" just to get the ship off the ground? Or do we assemble it in lunar orbit, far off, inconvenient lunar orbit, to which everything will have to be very expensively ferried?

Next: flight testing the ship. Add a few more billion dollars for that. Outfitting the ship, putting on the finishing touches that will transform a hollow steel hull into an environment: more billions. And finally, shuttling the passengers and crew, first to a briefing center in an orbiting space colony (don't forget to include the price of building and staffing that), and then to the waiting craft. Slap on, what? Maybe another six or seven billion?

The total cost of a single spacefaring adventure is staggering—not impossible, just staggering—and at the present time, no government is going to agree to finance one. So the scientists and rocket engineers, the star jockeys and dreamers, have occasionally fallen back on cheap scare tactics in an effort to win money for their cause.

Don't get too comfortable, they advise. Earth could go at any moment. This place is a mine field, and we have placed the mines. It began with the industrial revolution when we discovered how to make our lives better with coal and oil. We invented the automobile, the assembly line, the sprawling plant with its tall smokestacks vomiting black death into the atmosphere. We manufactured compounds and chemicals and foolishly stored their waste products in big metal drums. But there is oxygen in our atmosphere, and as the years passed, the metal turned to rust. The drums began to leak. Gradually, they offered up their poisonous contents to the land.

In the 1940s, we split some atoms. Then we split some more. One day we would use all this fantastic energy to power hair dryers and superboosted stereo systems. But now click, click, click go the Geiger counters, measuring the hundreds of hot spots in Nevada, in Russia, on half-forgotten atolls in the Pacific Ocean. Someday the trees will return. The plants will come too, but nobody will be able to eat them for a long, long time.

Steadily, methodically, almost, we are wrecking this once fair and friendly planet. The air is hazy and gray and hangs like an atomic cloud over the cities. The water tastes funny. Global temperatures are rising, scattering drought and floods that dry out the crops and wash away the houses. And the ozone layer has a hole in it.

So the engineers offer up their designs for massive spaceships. Just in case . . .

And some scientists hear the dinosaurs calling to us from far, far away. They listen to the tragic story of a master race of giants who endured for millions of years, only to be blasted off the Earth by some errant meteor.

"It could happen again, you know," say the paleontologists, and the astronomers, and the surveyors of rocks. "The solar system is full of junk. A direct hit would gouge a hole and raise a cloud and erase the sun and break the food chain and send us to the place where the dinosaurs are. It is wise to be prepared. We'd better build some ships."

And the star jockeys see into the future when the sun sputters and gasps and finally bursts apart in exhaustion. "We have to have ships," they say, "to carry humankind to a safe harbor."

These are the disaster scenarios. They are, at best, farfetched. True, the Earth is a little messy, and if we really try, we can completely destroy it for ourselves. But if we really try, we can also fix it. Earth is a highly efficient recycling center. It knows what to do to keep itself clean. Now *we* have to learn.

And why are we so worried about meteors smashing into us? Little ones arrive all the time, practically on a daily basis. True, a meteor was probably responsible for annihilating the dinosaurs, but the dinosaurs had been walking around trouble-free for well over a hundred million years. That's not a bad safety record. Besides, what makes us think ours is the only planetary system that gets hit by meteors? Wouldn't we be just as vulnerable somewhere else?

And as far as the sun going nova is concerned, don't give it another thought. Astronomers assure us that the sun has nothing exciting planned for the next several billion years. Do we really need those rocket ships right now?

Come on, tell us the real reason why you want to travel so far, through the blackness and the void and the cold, cold silence of space. Tell us why you dream the dreams of rocketmen.

If you have come with me all this way, you already know the answer.

Listen.

When the night is dark and clear and the winter winds are silent, you can hear them. You can hear the stars. The great red one in Orion, the white one in Auriga, the doubles and triples, the flame throwers and gravity ghosts. The two thousand you can see, the billions and countless billions that are really there, farther away than you can ever imagine. They have voices that float through the spaceblack and land on your ears.

Listen.

If you have ever wondered what Venus looks like under those pale sulphuric acid clouds, or if Barnard's star really has planets, or if anybody out there is wondering about us, then you know why we have to build some ships. We have to see it all for ourselves. In person. In space suits, maybe, or through the windows of a great lumbering ship. But right out there, with human fingers close enough to touch the methane shores and hydrogen seas. With fingers close enough to touch other fingers. Out there, with the stars.

Greetings from the Tin Man

It was the early 1970s, and we had ourselves a target. The Russians had picked it, although God knows why. It was Venus. Venus, similar to us in size and mass, had long been thought of as Earth's sister planet. Ha! Evil twin is more like it. About the only nice thing you can say about Venus is that it has a surface. But what a surface! Ground temperatures are well in excess of 700 degrees, making it hot enough to melt, not only the cheese on a pizza, but the metal pizza pan as well. The pressure rivals that found at the bottom of the

NASA/JPL

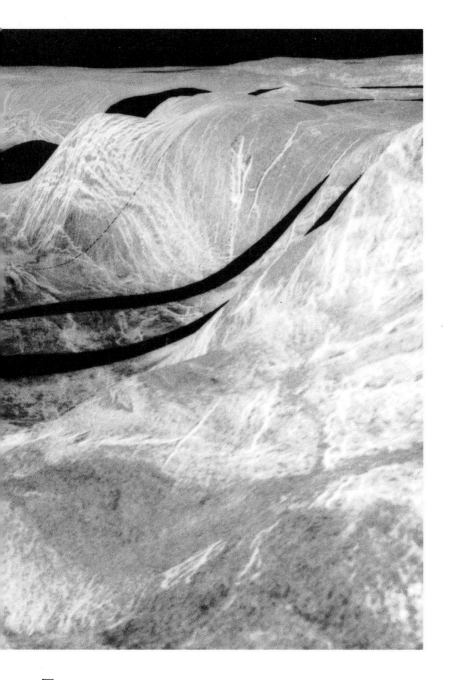

*T*he eerie terrain of Ishtar Terra on Venus photographed by the radar eyes of the Magellan *spacecraft*

deepest trench in the Pacific Ocean, and the atmosphere reeks of stinking gases. And to top it off, a fine mist of sulphuric acid sprinkles the land. Nice choice for one of our first times out.

Well, we obviously couldn't send humans to Venus, so we sent tin men instead; we sent probes. In Russian the tin men were called *Venera*. They were small and tough, but apparently not tough enough. Almost all of them were crushed like paper cups as they descended through the heavy cloud layers. The ones that actually made it to the surface lasted only about an hour before they joined their comrades in space probe heaven. Some rotten little planet this Venus!

A few years later we built new tin men. In 1978 a little craft named *Pioneer-Venus 1* fell into orbit around the cloud-shrouded planet. We had given the orbiter Superman eyes so it could peer through the gloom all the way down to the surface. It carried special cameras to record what it saw, and slowly, we began to learn the truth about Venus.

Sitting upon a "continent" the size of Australia is Venus's largest mountain, Maxwell Montes, significantly taller than Mount Everest. There is no water, and the planet is cracked and scarred and dotted by volcanoes. Venusian winds blow gently, hardly eroding an ancient landscape. The atmosphere is almost pure carbon dioxide.

The scientists sighed and wished for radar eyes just like the tin men had. They wished for strong-hulled ships. They wished for space suits and helmets made of impossible fabrics so they could walk around on Ishtar Terra and climb the slopes of Rhea Mons. But alas, the scientists had to stay home, jealously listening to the probes and orbiters tell of their adventures.

And then there was Mars. We are in love with Mars. It is red and rocky, and it has spectacular pink sunsets. It has gentle white polar caps just like Earth and a summertime equatorial temperature that can hit 60 degrees Fahrenheit. But more than that, Mars has a network of long, winding channels that twist and turn tantalizingly across the dry, dusty surface. *What are they?* we have asked ourselves over and over. And the *Mariner* photographs whisper back: *Perhaps they are dried-out riverbeds.* Perhaps, once upon a long, long time ago, Mars had flowing water. Perhaps Mars once had life.

What Viking *saw as it approached the planet Mars. At the top of the picture is Olympus Mons, Mars's largest volcano. Also visible is a thin layer of frost.*

NASA/JPL

Viking *digs into the Martian soil looking for signs of life.*
NASA/JPL

In 1976 we sent the tin man to Mars. We called it *Viking.* We should have gone ourselves. *Viking* dutifully sifted through the salmon-colored sand, testing and tasting and searching for the life we so desperately wanted to find. Back home the scientists waited. Their hearts were in their throats, but their souls were 38 million miles away.

The days dragged on. *Viking* sent pictures. It was wild and beautiful up there and hauntingly familiar. Like somewhere in Arizona. The scientists swooned. "If only we had been able to go . . ."

And then it was message day.

DATA COMING THROUGH . . . *Viking* screamed across the planetgap.

TEST RESULTS ON LIFE EXPERIMENT . . .

The scientists and engineers leaned in. The biologists craned their necks. Somewhere a second hand swept a clock face, measuring the Earth seconds. Data bits and data bits and data bits rushed home at the speed of light.

. . . TESTS INCONCLUSIVE . . .

And the silence of disbelief crashed like a wave in the room.

The scientists' hearts exploded in frustration. The years of work, the dedication, the sleepless nights and anxiety-filled days had all come down to an "inconclusive."

Slowly, they filed from the room. "We shouldn't have sent the tin man," they said. "Tin men aren't alive. They can't

Red and rocky like the American Southwest, Mars tantalizes us. Did Martians once crawl across this wild, dry landscape? Viking's soil tests were inconclusive.

NASA/JPL

touch the ground and feel the life beneath the sand. They can't look at the riverbeds and see the shadows of the bones. They can't hear the voices of the Martians."

The scientists said thank you to a tired *Viking*, which had done its work well. "But still," they whispered, "we should have gone ourselves."

N Is for Alien

Something's fishy.

A cloud wisp edges toward a yellow full moon, and the astronomers slowly scan the sky. A meteor falls, trailing chips of red. The night breathes like a sleeper.

"Where are they?" whisper the astronomers.

Somewhere an owl calls, its head swiveling half turns in the darkness.

But no one answers the astronomers, so they ask their question again.

The night remains still and silent except for the owl.

The astronomers think that something is fishy.

Once upon a time the philosophers told us we were special. The sun revolved around us, they said. The stars rose and set for us. But then came the revolution. Gradually we realized we were just another little dot in a universe filled with dots. Unless you stood very, very close, you couldn't even see us out there among the stars. And so it does not seem possible that this nowhere, nothing, nondescript little planet of ours can be the only one with life. Surely there must be others. . . .

Virtually all our mythologies tell of strange little beings with fabulous powers. In some stories, the beings simply appear; in others, they arrive in what sounds suspiciously like flying ships. But it was not until the mid-1940s that the idea of alien life really began to take hold.

The 1940s saw what UFOlogists call a major "flap," a flurry of reported sightings of unidentified flying objects. Since then, the number of reports has grown so large that the air force, the government, and local sheriffs' departments are quite frankly sick to death of them. (Through the years it has been their job to take down the information and conduct investigations.) While the vast majority of these UFOs have been explained away as planets, weather balloons, lights on the undersides of blimps, clouds, and other perfectly Earth-normal phenomena, a handful of cases remain unsolved. This is not to say that the aliens have arrived, but in its own way, it leaves us with something to think about.

For more than seventy years we have been broadcasting our presence to the universe. The messages have been strange; radio plays of "The Lone Ranger," episodes of "Amos and Andy," Superbowl games, Kennedy's assassination, the Miss America Pageant, our landing on the moon. These pictures have long since evaporated, but the words are traveling, streaming outward on scores of radio frequencies to the Orion nebula and beyond. All you need to hear us is a radio telescope, aimed in our direction and set to our broadcast band.

But this is no way to talk to aliens. It is incidental chatter, overheard conversations, bits and pieces scattered here and there that say a lot about us but nothing about our intentions. Even if someone has found us and is listening, will he or she or it be able to make any sense of Rocky and Bullwinkle? Do we even want some far advanced civilization to know us as moose and squirrel?

In 1960 astronomer Frank Drake finally got the go-ahead for the ambitious and exciting Project Ozma. Named for the beautiful princess of the mythical land of Oz, Ozma was established to search for intelligent signals from outer space. Drake knew it was the longest of long shots. He had one telescope, the radio dish* at Green Bank, West Virginia, so he could listen to only one star at a time. And because it was radio, Drake could listen to only one frequency at a time. But even more demoralizing was the distinct possibility that nobody was transmitting. Maybe they were all listening, hoping to pick up the other guy's message. In short, Drake was looking for a needle in a haystack, a needle he wasn't even sure was there.

But suppose it was . . .

To boost his odds, Drake selected his targets very carefully. Evidence seemed to suggest that two nearby stars, Epsilon Eridani and Tau Ceti, each had at least one dark orbiting body, possibly a planet. Although this was certainly better than a star with no planets, it was hardly a guarantee. To a curious alien, our sun might seem like a hot prospect; after all, it's got nine planets, practically a bonanza. But just look at the choices. Four of them are big gaseous blobs without even so much as a solid surface. One planet is frozen solid, two are pizza ovens, and one, Mars, is a frustratingly near miss. So the results for our solar system are: intelligent life-bearing planets—11 percent.

Does that mean one out of nine planets in the universe has intelligent life? No. It simply means that Earth was in the right place at the right time, and it doesn't take much to knock a planet out of the running. Had we been just a few million miles closer to the sun, we might have become like Venus. A few million miles farther and we are Mars, without an atmosphere and without water.

---

*Radio telescopes are fondly called dishes because they look like giant shallow soup bowls.

Scientists call our position in the solar system the *life zone*. Aptly named, the life zone is the very narrow band around a star that provides the best conditions for life to arise. Are the planets thought to be circling Epsilon Eridani and Tau Ceti inside the life zone? We have no idea, but Drake figured these two stars probably offered him his best shot. At least he wasn't aiming at a black hole.

So Drake turned on the telescope's clock drive and waited. The weeks passed. For Ozma's assigned time period each day, the dish at Green Bank collected the blips and crackles and crunchy static pouring from a not-so-silent universe. It was the mindless noise of stars in turmoil, the primal junk of gas clouds and nebulae.

Drake sifted through the printouts looking for a pattern, hoping to find a recurring code of some sort. Anything that could be converted to binary language and then into a picture. Anything that looked as though it had been deliberately sent. But the universe is big, and the stars are almost endless in number, and Drake heard nothing but the howling winds of space.

Project Ozma lasted only a few months. The grant givers had had enough. "Waste of time!" they said and snapped their wallets shut.

But Drake and several other astronomers refused to give up. They nickel and dimed it and managed to scrape together funds to keep up the search, although it was no longer called Project Ozma. Now the operation was referred to as SETI, the Search for Extraterrestrial Intelligence, and Europe had joined in the hunt. In the Soviet Union, scientists at the Gorky Radiophysical Institute scanned the heavens, hoping for the success that had eluded Drake and his team. They too came up empty, although they still continue to search.

The SETI astronomers have not had it easy. Funding for

the project has been less than spectacular and was withdrawn a number of times.[†] Many people see SETI as a hairbreadth away from Little Green Men and flying saucers. They imagine the spindly-legged monsters from *War of the Worlds* and every slime glob from every grade B movie ever made. But what if another life form is really out there?

In 1961 Frank Drake came up with an extraordinary equation. It was Drake's formula for determining how many intelligent civilizations exist right now in the universe. The equation considers seven factors, all of which are multiplied together to yield a single number, N—the number of advanced life forms with whom we might make contact.

$$N = R^* f_p n_e f_l f_i f_c L$$

The Drake formula can be frighteningly cruel or sublimely generous because it depends almost entirely on guesswork. Where a pessimist can make N a very small number, an optimist can boost it into the several millions. For instance, R^* is the number of stars in the galaxy. This we think we know, but f_p represents the fraction of stars that have planets. This we don't know—although then again, maybe we do. Certainly one star in the Milky Way has planets—ours—and there are an estimated one hundred billion stars in our galaxy. Turning that into a fraction, we get

$$f_p = 1/100,000,000,000$$

[†]On Columbus Day in 1992, NASA was finally granted the funds for SETI that it so desperately wanted. Amid fanfare and great cheering, two massive radio telescopes—one in the Mojave Desert and the other at Arecibo, Puerto Rico—moved into position to listen for alien voices. So, as of this writing, the search is still on—and better than ever before.

But is that the number we should use? Most scientists say no. It should be larger. How large? We guess.

Another unknown is n_e, the average number of Earthlike planets. How many of those do we know about? Again, only one, so what do we do? Do we shove 1 into the equation or go with something bigger, assuming that any day now we'll find more planets?

The guessing goes on. f_l is the fraction of planets where life can actually develop. In our solar system, it's one in 9 or 11 percent, but does that percentage hold true for the entire universe?

f_i is the fraction of systems with intelligent life. Obviously, just because something can reproduce doesn't mean it can also build spaceships and control nuclear energy. So on how many planets did the amino acids turn into rocket scientists?

f_c is the fraction of species who can and want to communicate with us. What do you think? All of them? Maybe none of them. Maybe they have found that communicating with other civilizations is disastrous. Strangers come to your planet, mess up your ecology, boss you around, and spread disease. Hey, who needs it? If that's the case, then $f_c = 0$.*

And finally we have L, the average life span of an intelligent civilization. Again, the only civilization we know about is ours, and we have not even lasted as long as the dodo. Furthermore, at what point is a civilization considered intelligent? When they build their first radio? When they split the atom? When they achieve space travel? Or when they achieve peace? To date, our life span would then be 70 years, 50 years, 20 years, or 0. Let's hope someone else is doing better than we are.

---

*Strictly speaking, this number can't be zero because when everything is multiplied together, N will wind up equaling 0. And if N = 0, where do we fit in?

So what are the results of the Drake equation? How many civilizations are out there, hoping, perhaps, for a phone call from Earth? Astronomer George Abell is optimistic. His N is an incredible 10 billion! That would put another intelligent life-form within three hundred light-years of us—within range of physical contact.

Plainly, we could not head out in the kiddie car rockets that are presently in our garage. Even if we managed to build one of those lumbering space arks, it would be scores of generations before we could get anywhere near the target planet. Would you go? While the prospect of standing face-to-(hopefully)-face with an alien would be a big draw for many of us, the reality is that the original people who signed on would not be the ones to arrive.

But suppose we conquer the mysteries of the near-light-speed ship. Suppose Dr. Bussard builds his ramjet, or one morning, like a bolt out of the blue, a tall, bearded mathematician yells, "Oh, great, glorious googolplex! I've done it!" and comes up with a fabulous star drive.

Christen the ship *Einstein's Promise*. Now we are streaming through space at 99.999 percent c. Time dilation has kicked in and is shaving centuries off the journey. The aliens wait, three hundred light-years away, on a planet with a breathable atmosphere and vast bodies of water. Their double suns shine softly orange in a sky only slightly different from the one we see. Their eyes, deep as space itself and gently almond-shaped, watch for the lightship from Earth.

Back home, the millennia will pass. Countries will rise and fall and nations will jockey for position. Life will inevitably go on. . . .

Six years ship time and maybe a few months. That's all it will take. We can be there, stepping from a door, a hatch, a

23 SQUARES

73 SQUARES

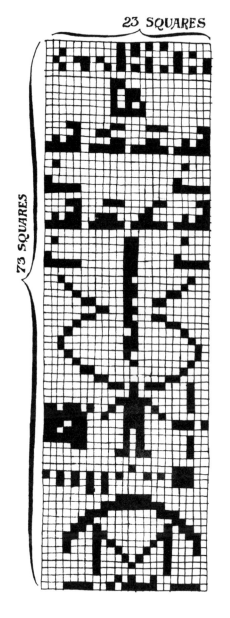

Frank Drake and Carl Sagan designed this binary message for any aliens who might be listening. If the aliens can break the binary code, the message becomes a picture describing our Solar System, our DNA structure, and us (the little figure near the bottom). Drake's historic message was sent from the Arecibo radio telescope in Puerto Rico. We're still waiting for an answer.

lighted corridor into the science fiction novels we wrote so long ago.

The almond eyes will follow us from our world into theirs. A hand will reach out to touch. A moment, poised, like an angel on the head of a pin.

"We come from a place called Earth," we will whisper. "A blue planet with a yellow sun. It's not very far."

They will not know our words, but they will know our souls, for they too will have been waiting, wondering if they were all alone.

The wind will move the sand, and the water will stroke the shore. Meteors will fall and comets will shake their golden heads. And one day the great ships will rise from the third planet on the left to join with the angels as they make their star crossing. ★

BIBLIOGRAPHY

BOOKS

Adelman, Saul J., and Benjamin Adelman. *Bound for the Stars.* Englewood Cliffs, N.J.: Prentice-Hall, 1981.

Aldiss, Brian. *Trillion Year Spree: The History of Science Fiction.* New York: Atheneum, 1986.

————. *Billion Year Spree: The True History of Science Fiction.* New York: Doubleday, 1973.

Brosnan, John. *Future Tense: The Cinema of Science Fiction.* New York: St. Martin's Press, 1978.

Goswami, Amit. *The Cosmic Dancers.* New York: Harper and Row, 1983.

Gunn, James. *Alternate Worlds: The Illustrated History of Science Fiction.* Englewood Cliffs, N.J.: Prentice-Hall, 1975.

Herbert, Nick. *Faster than Light, Superluminal Loopholes in Physics.* New York: New American Library, 1988.

Kaufmann, William J., III. *The Cosmic Frontiers of General Relativity.* Boston: Little, Brown, 1977.

Kavaler, Lucy. *Freezing Point.* New York: John Day, 1970.

Lilley, Sam. *Discovering Relativity for Yourself.* Cambridge: Cambridge University Press, 1981.

Macvey, John W. *Time Travel.* Chelsea, Mich.: Scarborough House, 1990.

Mallove, Eugene. *The Starflight Handbook.* New York: John Wiley and Sons, 1989.

Menville, Douglas, and R. Reginald. *Things to Come: An Illustrated History of the Science Fiction Film.* New York: New York Times Books, 1977.

Nicholson, Iain. *The Road to the Stars.* New York: William Morrow, 1978.

Scholes, Robert. *Structural Fabulation.* Notre Dame: University of Notre Dame Press, 1975.

Shklovskii, Iosif S. *Stars: Their Birth, Life, and Death.* San Francisco: W. H. Freeman, 1978.

Strong, James. *Flight to the Stars.* New York: Hart, 1965.

PERIODICALS

Baker, Sherry. "Human Hibernation." *Omni*, March 1984, 70–74.

Ben-Abraham, Avi. "Putting Death on Ice." *The Saturday Evening Post*, April 1989, 60–62, 111.

Bova, Ben. "Star Blazers." *Omni*, Dec. 1984, 22.

Bussard, R. W. "Galactic Matter and Interstellar Flight," *Astronautica Acta* 6 (1960): 13, 180–194.

"Cold Storage." *Scientific American*, February 1990, 22.

Freedman, David H. "Cosmic Time Travel." *Discover*, June 1989, 58–64.

McKinley, John M., and Paul Doherty. "In Search of the 'Starbow': The Appearance of the Starfield from a Relativistic Spaceship." *American Journal of Physics* 47 (April 1979): 309–315.

Moskowitz, Saul. "Visual Aspects of Trans-Stellar Space Flight." *Sky and Telescope*, May 1967, 290–294.

Sanger, Ing. E. "Some Optical and Kinematical Effects in Interstellar Astronautics." *Journal of the British Interplanetary Society* 18 (1961–62): 273–277.

Scobia, William. "Ice to Ashes, Dust to Dust." *Macleans*, May 12, 1980, 31–32.

Sheldon, E., and R. H. Giles. "Celestial Views from Non-Relativistic Interstellar Spacecraft." *Journal of the British Interplanetary Society* 36 (1983): 99–114.

Simets, R. W., and E. Sheldon. "The Celestial View from a Relativistic Starship." *Journal of the British Interplanetary Society* 34 (1981): 83–99.

"Toward the Conquest of Death: Science Mounts a Massive Assault on the Grim Reaper." *The Futurist*, Dec. 1980, 71–77.

Warner, Nora. "Hibernation of Black Bears May Aid in Space Travel." *Science Digest*, Sept. 1979, 20–23.

INDEX